OCEAN BLUE

Noelene Jenkinson

Chapter 1

Sophie Brookfield longed to get out to Jewel Island on the Great Barrier Reef and begin her research work. She had left Sydney Airport two hours earlier and just landed in Cairns. What did they say of Queensland? Beautiful one day, perfect the next.

She paced the airport lounge, anxious to escape this public place where she might be recognised or found. Not because of her familiar socialite face, but in case her father carried out his threat and tried to stop her fulfilling her dream. If the helicopter pilot ever arrived! What could be taking him so long?

She brushed aside a wisp of glossy, chestnut hair and picked up a women's magazine, forcing herself to sit down and flip through its gossipy pages. Not really her cup of tea. Poring over copies of National Geographic or Outback magazine was more to her liking. But within minutes, constantly distracted to scour the crowds for the tardy pilot, she gave up, heaved a sigh, and impatiently replaced the magazine.

She checked her watch. He was extremely late. She scowled, hoping there was no misunderstanding about time. Two weeks earlier on the telephone, the island receptionist had assured her the pilot would meet her inside the building at her arrival gate. Exactly where she sat now, hot and irritable, and longing for a swim.

Edgy, she tapped her feet and distractedly drummed her fingers on her suitcase. Thirty minutes and a bottle of chilled water later, Sophie still waited, with no sign of her pilot and a growing desperation to be gone. She had checked the airport information desk and been reassured *Seascape Airways* always personally met their clients.

Sophie had no choice but to stay put, but not for much longer. Cooling her heels for almost an hour had blackened her mood. The man better have a convincing explanation. Five minutes more, she vowed, and he would lose her business.

As if from her thoughts, a uniformed

vision in white suddenly materialised. He stared in her direction and Sophie's hopes lifted. She raised her eyebrows in questioning hope and the man strode purposefully forward.

She forgot to be stern because she was so captivated by the sun-browned man and his devastating smile that her anger vanished. Even at her above average height she was forced to tilt her gaze upward to meet his dark laughing eyes. Firm muscles flexed through his crisp, white pilot's uniform, while navy and white epaulettes spanned his broad shoulders.

'Miss Brookfield?' He inclined his head of sandy hair, his voice as warm and smooth as the tropical air.

'Mr Mitchell?' Sophie enquired curtly.

He extended a hand. 'Call me Drew.' His mischievous eyes flickered freely over her willowy frame.

She ignored his outstretched hand and cordiality, stubbornly reaching for her suitcase instead. 'You're late.'

'My apologies.'

No explanation, she noted. Instead, he leaned across and firmly swept the luggage from her grasp.

'What kept you?' Sophie demanded.

As his huge brown hands and her slender fingers brushed together, he murmured, 'Another beautiful lady actually.'

Sophie privately groaned. A womaniser. She knew the type. Well, he would soon discover this trip was strictly work.

This time his sparkling gaze moved slowly upward from her sandalled feet, absorbing her shape inside the cream linen skirt with a front split, across her blue cropped T-shirt and rested on the glossy hair that brushed her shoulders, tamed by a silver barrette at her nape.

Worldly-wise but caught unaware and embarrassed by the deep, raking stare, Sophie dropped her lashes and blushed, picking at an imaginary thread on her skirt. 'I'm ready to leave,' she pointed out crisply.

'No hurry. We take things easy up here.'

'Arriving one hour late isn't taking it easy,' Sophie retorted. 'It's rude.'

She pushed on a pair of sunglasses as if they could be a shield against him but his disturbing brown eyes penetrated her cool.

'The delay was...unavoidable.'

I'll bet, she thought, maddened that this intensely masculine creature threw her completely off-balance, making her feel inadequate and unsettled.

An admirable achievement considering her private education and that a large part of her adult life had been spent in the public eye. Her father considered it good public relations, but Sophie deemed it an intrusion.

The reason she had opted out in recent years to create a life of her own against her father's hopes and wishes, and the reason she was here today. Her thesis research was just one step further along in pursuit of her dream.

Drew stepped aside and indicated an exit. 'If you'd care to follow me.'

Even Sophie's long legs struggled to keep up with the powerful giant bearing her luggage as they walked outside into a burst of warm, tropical sunshine and across the tarmac to the waiting helicopter. Drew opened the cockpit door, heaved Sophie's case inside then caught her hand and helped her up.

Flustered by his touch, she unwillingly mumbled, 'Thank you.'

He restrained a grin. 'My pleasure.'

Sophie watched him walk around the front, retrieve sunglasses from his uniform pocket, push them on and run a large brown hand fluidly through his hair. He was so cool and controlled, whereas she felt unusually ruffled.

Mitchell eased into the cockpit beside her and strapped himself in. After radio contact with the control tower, he flicked some switches and the blades above slowly rotated into life.

As the noise and power grew, his large hands eased on the controls and they lifted off, tilting away from the airport and out over the dazzling, crystal waters of the Coral Sea. Sophie felt a surge of adrenalin.

Having studied the region, she experienced the eerie sensation of coming home. She knew this was the largest complex of coral reefs and islands in the world, covering an area larger than Great Britain, stretching 2000 kilometres from New Guinea and down the east Australian coast.

It harboured an astonishing diversity and abundance of sea life and thousands of species of fish. Being a marine national park, it was also the breeding ground for many rare and endangered species. Whales came to the warm waters from the Antarctic to give birth to their young, and six of the world's seven species of turtle bred here. The latter being the focus of her thesis, and the reason for her work and this visit.

Further out, the Pacific Ocean would be crashing in over the outer reef, a natural rampart protecting the Queensland coast. But between the coastline and the outer barrier lay the tranquil island-studded pristine waters of the inner reef.

Down there, she thought as she gazed, coral polyps flourished in the warm sea currents and Sophie eagerly anticipated her forthcoming work. Enthralled and intoxicated by the magnificent view, she finally relaxed.

Perhaps sensing her change of mood, Drew asked, 'What's your name?'

She sighed. There was no need for him to know but it was unavoidable. After they landed, he would fly off and they would never meet again. Unless he was scheduled to fly her back to the mainland when she left.

Feeling mean if she withheld, she decided to oblige. 'Sophie.'

He grinned. 'Nice. Here on holidays?'

'Work,' she corrected his natural assumption. 'How long before we arrive?'

'Fifteen minutes. What kind of work?'

'I'm a marine biologist.'

Mitchell raised his bushy eyebrows. 'I'm impressed.'

'That wasn't my intention. I've come to study the green turtles among other sea life.'

'Incredible. I'll call you Flipper!'

Sophie privately sighed and turned her gaze away and down to the seemingly endless inspiring ocean beneath them.

'Spectacular, isn't it?' Mitchell enthused.

She nodded without comment, reluctant to agree with anything he said.

'It's so vast. Did you know it's visible from the moon?' She nodded. 'Where will you be researching?'

Sophie shrugged. 'It depends.'

'On what?'

'How well my local guide knows the area.'

Her announcement appeared to intrigue him for one side of his mouth edged into the hint of a grin. Sophie suspected his dark eyes were laughing at her behind his sunglasses and wondered why.

Conversation lapsed until Jewel Island appeared in the blue-green ocean ahead, a dark green circle of lush tropical growth edged by a perimeter of white sand and shallow patch reefs.

Chosen because it was small and isolated, and therefore potentially private, its waters shaded from pale transparent green offshore to royal blue further out, Sophie welled with delight. Perfect. Flashy overcrowded resorts weren't her style.

Suddenly, the helicopter dipped forward and dropped at joy-ride speed, swooping down towards the island. For an instant, Sophie panicked, thinking they were about to crash.

'What's the matter?' She gripped the edge of her seat.

Drew's cheeks dimpled as he buzzed the treetops. 'Just letting them know we've arrived.'

Sophie gasped, utterly speechless, her heart thumping. As they banked to the right and descended, she burned with resentment at Drew's reckless move and only breathed easily again when he settled the chopper safely on the beach.

In relieved and frosty silence, Sophie

alighted. Holding on to her sandals and her private rage, she marched off across the warm sand, following a pathway perfumed with the heady fragrance of gardenia and frangipani directed by signposts that led her all the way to Reception. Drew trailed behind with her luggage.

They were greeted by an attractive brunette with an enviable golden tan. 'Welcome to Jewel,' she said cheerfully.

Appearing behind her, Drew set down Sophie's case, leaned forward over the desk and kissed the receptionist on the cheek.

In a heartbeat, all of Sophie's idle fantasies were dashed. Unaware that she had secretly harboured any at all, she felt as if someone had just stabbed a pin into her favourite birthday balloon or broken a favourite toy, and reeled in shock at the discovery.

'This is Miss Sophie Brookfield.' Drew introduced her with pointed formality.

'J.B. Brookfield's daughter?' The woman's gaze widened. Sophie nodded.

'Wow. Pleased to meet you,' she gushed, as though in the presence of royalty.

'She's actually come to the island to work,' Drew teased.

'That's right. You're a marine biologist, aren't you?'

'Almost.' Sophie managed a weak smile, feeling an intruder between these two who, judging by their obvious bond of affection, were more than casual friends.

'I'm Stephanie Thomas and you're to ask me for absolutely anything while you're here. You'll find the bar and restaurant in the Cabana Lounge further around the pathway by the pool.' She handed a key to Sophie. 'You're in Bungalow Seven. I know you'll enjoy your stay with us because this island lives up to its name and is a gem in paradise.'

She turned to Drew, lounging easily against the desk. 'You were later than expected. Everything okay?'

'Sure.' He glanced at Sophie. 'I'll explain later.'

Sensing her cue to leave, she reached for her suitcase but it was swiftly seized and her gaze levelled with Drew's dusky brown eyes.

'I can manage.'

'No trouble,' he assured her warmly. 'Besides, I know the way to Bungalow Seven.'

Sophie followed him past the thatched cocktail bar he idly referred to as the watering hole and a sculptured lagoon pool with a central waterfall surrounded by glossy tropical greenery.

Outside her bungalow, purple bougainvillaea rambled over a sheltered entry patio forming a small, secluded courtyard. Drew stepped aside as Sophie unlocked her door.

Inside, she gasped. Ignoring the sumptuous furnishings of natural pine and bright tropical prints, she was drawn to a wall of windows at the far end that revealed glassy blue waters rippling gently onto the beach only metres away across the sand.

'Heaven,' Sophie breathed, then half turned. 'I don't suppose you know who my local guide might be?'

She sensed Drew's hesitation as his shoulders hunched into an easy shrug. His lazy grin was slow in coming, filling her mind with suspicion.

'You're looking at him.'

Sophie stared, her pale blue eyes wide. 'You!' She closed her gaping mouth and collected her thoughts. 'Why didn't you say?'

'We didn't exactly get off on the right foot, did we? And you're still angry with me for being late.'

"Rightly so,' she said in sharp defence.

'I thought you would have cooled off by now.'

Sophie tensed. 'I'm perfectly cool.'

'Maybe after you've had a dip in the ocean,' he suggested with a wink.

Sophie ignored his quip, aware she still bore resentment. 'Are you the only guide available on the island?' Her inference was clear.

'Afraid so.' He arched one dark brow. 'Is that a problem?'

Sophie shuffled uncomfortably, suddenly realising how much time she was destined to spend with this disconcerting male. Which should not have bothered her because he was now clearly out of bounds and, besides, she was here to concentrate on her research.

'I'm not sure we can work together.'

'That's because you've decided you don't like me,' he teased.

Cornered, Sophie asked, 'You have the time for two jobs?'

'For you, I'll make the time,' he

murmured, swift and urbane. 'I have a partner.'

Sophie wondered if he meant the stunning Stephanie at Reception or someone else. If only he would wipe that wretched smile off his face. It was most disarming. He really was a charmer and a flirt. He already had a girlfriend but was coming on to her.

She released a private and disappointed sigh. He was just like all the others. After a quick catch or, worse, the Brookfield money.

Faced with a dilemma, Sophie accepted there was no one else to help her on the island and she didn't have time to find another. Drew Mitchell was it. She hoped the lovely Stephanie wasn't possessive because she and the boyfriend would be working together a lot. Sophie rubbed the back of her neck and dreamed of a swim.

Seeing her weary action, Drew said, 'I'll give you an hour to unwind then I'll show you around. Might even get in some snorkelling before dinner.'

'I can look around myself,' she objected.

'No bother. See you in an hour.'

He had turned on his heel and was gone

before she could protest further. Mitchell's arrogance niggled. He was so presumptuous. They would be seeing enough of each other and, not at all convinced that their working life would be harmonious, Sophie deemed any time spent apart was a good idea.

To her surprise as she unpacked, she heard the helicopter rotors beat into life. Through her windows, she glimpsed the aircraft rise from the sand and leave the island. Sophie frowned. Hadn't he promised to meet her? Surely he hadn't forgotten her already? The thought was humiliating. Or had he done it deliberately?

Optimistic, she waited. Impatiently. Longer than the hour until she conceded that he had stood her up. Finally, peeved at his snub and too tantalised to resist any longer, Sophie discarded her clothes, changed into a swimsuit and went along to the island pool. She dropped her towel onto a sun lounger and dived into the inviting water, stroking out a succession of laps in a vigorous crawl. She had left Sydney early this morning and missed her daily swim in their private heated pool at home.

Eventually, she drew herself out and reclined on the lounger, letting the sun's warmth soak away the droplets on her skin. As dusk approached, she returned to her bungalow and changed for dinner into a hugging shift of blue and mauve that intensified the colour of her eyes.

Sophie was just sliding her feet into heeled sandals when she heard the distinctive beating sound of the returning helicopter. Five minutes later, there was a knock at her door. Giving herself one final quick glance in the mirror, and annoyed that she tried to impress a man she wasn't even sure she completely trusted or respected yet, she ambled over to answer it.

Legs crossed, arms folded, he leant his muscled frame against the door. 'I know,' he raised his hands and an adorable, helpless smile, 'I'm late.'

He was so disgustingly neat and devastatingly handsome, all of her words of reproof flew out of her mind. There was something about a man in uniform, especially crisp white against tanned skin. Sophie understood why women found him irresistible. Herself included. And charm helped.

'So, what's new?'

His brows crinkled. 'Ouch!' He studied

her carefully. 'I'm sorry. Again.'

'Don't worry,' she said sweetly. 'It's obviously a habit. One I don't like but I guess I might have to adjust. Unless you're about to change?'

His smile faded. 'Actually, it couldn't be helped.'

'That's what you said last time.' And what did it matter? She had occupied herself perfectly well without him. 'I trust you plan on being more punctual when I start my work. I only have two weeks here so my time is limited and precious. I've come to work, not wait until you decide you're ready. I'm paying you good money to help me.'

The moment the last words were out, Sophie new they reeked of condescension, and she could have pinched herself for an uncharacteristic lack of tact. It seemed this frustrating man brought out the worst in her.

'The husband of the sick woman I flew back to Cairns has just offered me money, too.'

Checked by his announcement, she quickly recovered and said, 'The holy dollar is obviously more important to you than a promise.'

'I didn't take it,' he said quietly, 'but that's not the point. Get one thing straight, Flipper. You might be paying the bills but out here we play by my rules.'

She knew it. The man was impossible. They could never work together. And it irritated her no end when he used that silly nickname. 'In that case, I'll find a replacement.'

He caught hold of her arm. 'Sorry to break the news but there is no one else. Relax. And slow down.' A note of diplomacy edged into his voice. 'You've just arrived. There'll be plenty of time to achieve everything you want. In a few days, we'll be diving.'

Sophie was appalled. 'That long!' She had expected to begin her research tomorrow in case one of her father's minions located her. She struggled with the knowledge that J.B., her own flesh and blood, had forced her to such subterfuge.

Drew scowled at her tense impatience. 'We'll need to scout potential reefs first.'

Sophie sighed and allowed reason to prevail. He was right. The man obviously knew his business. 'Of course.'

'Let yourself go, Sophie,' Drew urged in a soothing voice. 'This is paradise, remember?'

His words caused her to pause and reflect. 'Yes, it is, isn't it?' she agreed, forced to forget outside pressures and her inner sense of urgency to appreciate her magnificent idyllic surroundings.

'To compensate for my unavoidable delays today, I'll take you to dinner.' He looked down at his uniform. 'If you don't mind waiting while I change.'

'Frankly, I'm fed up with waiting.' Sophie managed to reply with an edge of humour, determined to be politely open with him. 'I'm hungry.'

She walked past him and headed off along the scented overgrown pathway.

Drew caught up with her and fell into step alongside. 'Five minutes.' He held up a splayed hand. 'Promise.' When she hesitated, he added, 'There are things we need to discuss.'

'All right,' Sophie conceded, stifling a grin at his contrite expression. He looked positively boyish and, despite his casual air, really seemed to care what she thought. Maybe he wasn't as arrogant as she thought after all.

In her split second's inattention along the unfamiliar pathway, Sophie's foot caught in thick palm fronds and she stumbled against Drew. In immediate reaction, he shot an arm about her waist in support, drawing her up firmly against his chest bringing their faces alarmingly close.

Recovering, Sophie pushed herself away, every sense in her body on alert.

'Are you all right?' There was a new and unfamiliar softness in his voice.

'If you weren't in such a hurry,' she muttered ungraciously to cover her unease.

'You said you were hungry,' he teased.

His mouth curled into a mocking grin and his brown eyes roamed over her intently with more than casual interest.

'Hungry, not starving.' Ruffled, and feeling herself on the verge of a blush, Sophie broke free and strode ahead.

At the watering hole, Drew found her a stool at the polished wooden bar and addressed the waiter. 'Miss Brookfield will have an Island Cocktail, Sam.'

There he was again, being presumptuous. Glancing down at her black look, he quipped, 'Better make it a double.'

He patted her hand. 'Give me ten minutes.'

She found even that brief touch of his warm skin against hers utterly tantalising.

'One second later and I start without you.'

'Deal,' he grinned and disappeared.

Chapter 2

Sophie had barely finished her cocktail when Drew reappeared, his hair damp from what must have been a supersonic shower, wearing light slacks and a colourful shirt.

In full view as he approached, she deliberately checked her watch. 'Eleven minutes. You're improving.'

Drew's deep responding laugh was extremely sensual. Stephanie was one lucky female and would need to keep a close rein on this one. Sexy and dangerous were words that sprang to Sophie's mind.

'Like a refill?' He indicated her empty glass.

'No.' She slid from the stool. 'I'd prefer dinner.'

The Cabana Restaurant oozed tropical charm. From its thatched roof and gently pulsating ceiling fans overhead to the swathes of hibiscus and perfumed flowers, rustic timber tables and crisp white linen. Drew found them a table to one side favoured by a soft evening breeze.

Before they seated themselves, he said, 'Since it's a smorgasbord and you're so hungry, let's fill our plates first, shall we? Can't have you fainting on me.'

Sophie followed him and served herself from the sumptuous seafood, spoilt for choice from the buffet of fish, lobster and prawns laid out among platters of salad and juicy tropical fruits.

Back at their table, Drew asked, 'Wine?'

'I'd love another Island Cocktail,' Sophie admitted sheepishly.

Drew tactfully restrained his mirth and re-ordered for them both. When their drinks arrived, he reached over and clinked glasses. 'To a harmonious working relationship.'

Sophie tilted her head, dubious of the achievement and wondered how on earth they would accomplish it but gave a restrained hopeful nod. For a while, they concentrated on their delicious meal, making little conversation.

Finally, Drew said, 'Do you realise we haven't disagreed for five minutes?'

'Amazing.'

Sophie filled her fork again, covered by his direct stare. It had softened, somehow. Grown warmer and she suspected he had been watching her for much longer than she realised.

'About your work,' he said. 'Where would you like to start?'

Sophie set down her knife and fingered her glass, casting a valiant upward glance to look into his smooth brown eyes. 'I'll need to explore as much area as possible, especially closer inshore and along beaches.'

'No problem.' Drew shrugged and, having finished his meal, leaned back into his chair. 'I have a motor cruiser, the *Reef Lady*. After we've searched around Jewel, I'll take you further out.' Perhaps sensing Sophie's caution in the light of his unreliability so far, he added, 'My partner will pilot the chopper while we're out, so I'm all yours.'

Interesting thought. Despite his laid back nature, Sophie was reassured. He had obviously given their work together some thought.

'Presuming we find the turtles, I'll need to spend time observing and logging them.

Try to determine age, location and so on.'

'Shouldn't be a problem. Six of the seven species of turtle breed along the reef. We should find some females laying eggs and maybe some young hatchlings.'

Sophie found herself the subject of Drew's undivided attention and intense scrutiny.

'How on earth did you become interested in green turtles?' he asked with another of his incredulous smiles.

'I've always loved the sea and everything in it.'

'Why?'

Sophie shrugged. 'Maybe I was born with salt in my blood.'

When Drew laughed, Sophie felt a surge of warmth rush through her, surprised to suddenly discover this man so comfortable to be with when she had initially found it necessary to be on guard. But then, it was rare for anyone to share her interests and she felt encouraged to continue.

'As a girl, I constantly dragged home gritty, salty-smelling creatures, much to my father's exasperation and my mother's disgust. I was a tomboy,' she confessed.

'Flipper,' Drew murmured, 'I find it

extremely hard to believe you were ever anything less than intensely feminine.'

'I was,' she insisted.

His gaze lingered over her sparkling blue eyes, flushed face and slightly parted lips.

'Then it must be a case of the ugly duckling turning into a swan,' he drawled.

Sophie's beating heart was thrown into chaos. He sounded like he actually meant it. She wondered what Stephanie would think of her boyfriend showering compliments on another woman.

'How about some dessert, Flipper?' Drew interrupted her thoughts.

Jolted back to reality, Sophie nodded and they returned to the buffet.

'Have you always lived in Sydney?' Drew asked when they resumed eating.

'Yes.'

'Like it?'

It was a simple question to which she was compelled to give an honest reply. 'Not particularly.'

He raised interested eyebrows. 'What are your plans when you finish university?'

Sophie's gaze clouded. 'My father wants me to sit at a desk behind the glass walls of

Brookfield Tower. Become a sophisticated executive.' She popped a slice of pawpaw into her mouth.

He noted her change of mood and flashed her a warm smile. 'You have no yearning to be a sophisticated executive?'

Sophie scoffed. 'Hardly. More likely a beachcomber.'

He eyed her closely. 'Have you told him yet?'

All manner of memories, some unwanted and more unpleasant than others, came flooding back. Sophie ignored her dish of luscious tropical fruits and gazed thoughtfully at Drew across the table. His probing suggested she had done him an injustice. Drew Mitchell was far more perceptive than she realised.

'I tried joining the family company immediately I finished school. Pressure and obligation.' Sophie confessed with a shrug. 'It was for a reason, but I hated it. I was utterly miserable shuffling papers all day so I left. Father was devastated and furious. He begged me to return but when I declined, he refused to support my university study when I decided to pursue my dream of marine biology.'

'How did you manage?'

'I'm working part-time to put myself through. I started after I was 21 so I'm rather older than your average graduate.' She darted him a hesitant smile. 'My father has been trying to stop me ever since. He thinks I'll be deterred and forced to join him. He even caused trouble at the café where I work so I nearly lost my job.'

'The old villain,' Drew sympathised.

'Clutching at straws, really,' Sophie said. 'So I've had to plan this research time without his knowledge. He doesn't know I'm here and I'd prefer it remained that way. So if you hear anything suspicious, I'd value you keeping my secret.' She smiled weakly.

'By all means,' Drew agreed. 'What an appalling tyrant.'

'No human being has the right to control another,' she said firmly. 'A person's soul needs independence and freedom.'

'You really are a poor little rich girl, aren't you?' Drew said kindly.

'My family does have its moments, I'm afraid.'

Sophie noticed a new glimmer of respect in Drew's eyes for her struggle and felt all the more pleasure in her small achievement because of his unspoken admiration and approval.

'I think we're going to make a great team,' he observed and his dark eyes covered her fondly. 'Just be patient and trust me, and we'll do fine.'

'I'm prepared to work hard and complete my study as soon as possible. For obvious reasons.'

'Every day?'

'As I explained, I don't have time to waste, and you're being generously paid,' she reminded him.

He extended both arms in a helpless gesture. 'All right. I suppose your father works seven days a week, too?'

'Always has.'

'Why do you think we have weekends?' he chided. When she didn't answer, he added, 'To renew the mind and restore the soul. You should relax more and enjoy life.'

'I do!' Sophie disagreed. 'Anyway, you hardly have time for grass to grow under your feet either. Chartering boats and flying helicopters.'

'Ah.' He leant forward in his seat and a twinkle entered his eyes. 'But when I'm out on the *Reef Lady* or in the pilot's seat, it's not work. I'm doing what I love.'

Drew's tanned face spread into a lazy smile, making deep crinkles at the corners of his eyes. Sophie's pulse rate yet again took a giant leap. To rally her composure, she sipped her tropical tea.

Growing more inquisitive about the enigmatic man seated opposite, Sophie cleared her throat and gathered sufficient courage to ask, 'Have you lived in Queensland all your life?'

'No. Only for ten years. I was born in Darwin.'

'Why did you come here?'

'To live with a woman in Cairns.'

Judging by Drew's steady challenging gaze, Sophie suspected his blunt pronouncement was meant to shock and she felt a twist of envy.

'My grandmother,' he explained with a wry grin. 'An angel with a walking stick.'

A deep affection and respect filtered into his voice as he spoke.

'Do you still live with her?'

'Unofficially, I'm away most of the time.' A wistful look crossed his face. 'She's the youngest old lady I've ever met.' He glanced at Sophie. 'You'd like each other.'

Why on earth should he say that? Sophie couldn't see any relevance in his comment. She grew unsettled again and pushed back her chair.

'If you'll excuse me, I'd like to call it a night.'

A live four-piece band had started playing and the easy strains of their gentle music drifted on the night across the restaurant. Drew rose courteously as she stood. 'Care to dance before you go?'

'No,' she replied hastily, suddenly afraid of the soft seduction of the music and a tropical night, adding, 'Thank you,' to temper the crisp edge in her voice.

He followed her outside where garden lamps sparkled their soft light across the darkness and caused reflections in the island pool.

'Like a stroll on the beach?'

The disturbing tenderness in his tone made her heart ache with loneliness and she rubbed her arms against the unwanted sensation.

'It's been a long day.' She rejected him gently. 'I'll see you tomorrow.'

'Fair enough. See you in the morning, then.'

'Yes.'

Silence hung heavily between them on the warm night. Hesitant to end what had eventuated as an amiable evening, Sophie strolled away without further comment. She had almost reached her bungalow when she heard heavy footsteps behind.

She whirled around to see Drew dangling a key that glinted in the moonlight. 'You forgot to lock it earlier in your haste for dinner.' His face was wreathed in a devilish grin. Sophie reached out for it but he snatched it away. 'Not so fast. You haven't thanked me.'

Sophie heaved an impatient sigh. 'Thank you.'

He clicked his tongue. 'Not good enough. The keys for a kiss.

Sophie gasped in amazement. 'You're kidding!'

'Definitely not.'

'What about Stephanie?' she asked.

Drew frowned. 'She won't mind.'

The man had no sense of guilt or disloyalty at all. He really was a philanderer of the highest order. As the stunned thoughts raced through Sophie's head, Drew stepped closer and she realised he was serious.

Imprisoned beneath the flower-laden arbour outside her door, she steadied herself, intending to make the obligation as brief as possible. But, outsmarted, two strong arms circled her waist and persuasive lips seduced her mouth with practiced ease. When Drew finally released her, she reeled away.

He pressed the key into her palm and murmured, 'Goodnight, Flipper.'

Sophie thought she heard a soft chuckle as he walked away. Feeling chastened, abandoned even, that he considered his kiss nothing more than a joke, Sophie despaired of his brash behaviour. It would place tension on their working relationship, not to mention his unfaithfulness to Stephanie.

That night, sleep only came to her after much restless turning. Sophie woke at daylight and rose immediately, looking out across the calm tropical sea. The sky was still young and washed with pink, the warm air an inducement to swim.

There was no one else about, so she stroked out her usual laps in the pool alone before stretching out on her towel to dry. When the sun grew hotter, she returned to her bungalow and showered, letting the spray stream over her skin like a warm waterfall. She towelled her hair, left it damp and slipped on white shorts and a blue shirt.

After breakfast in her room, she heard whistling. Her door was ajar and Drew pushed it wider.

'Hi,' he greeted lightly with his usual grin. 'Ready?'

'Of course.'

She eyed him warily. His attitude suggested he had forgotten his kiss last night, whereas Sophie still reeled from its disturbing effect.

For an hour, they sauntered the beach around the island, Sophie enjoying the feel of soft white sand between her toes. Occasionally they wandered into the sea, treading carefully among the coral shallows. The reef was so close, Sophie already felt a part of it and impatience to begin her research resurfaced.

Drew discussed favoured beaches and sites the turtles were known to frequent in the locality. Because nesting colonies had been observed all along the Great Barrier Reef, Sophie was hopeful of finding one not too far away.

As the main buildings reappeared, she

noticed the helicopter missing and commented.

'It was flown back to Cairns last night,' Drew explained.

'By your co-pilot?'

He nodded. 'Mal Beasley. I've known him five years and he's a good mate. As I said last night, while you and I are out in the *Reef Lady*, he'll handle all flights for me. Interested in snorkelling?'

Excited by the prospect, Sophie held up a hand and spread out her fingers. 'Give me five minutes to change.'

'I'll fetch our gear. Don't be late,' he quipped as a parting shot.

Don't be late, Sophie muttered, as she raced back to the bungalow and tugged on a pale blue swimsuit, caught her hair up in a thick knot and sped back to the beach.

Drew was waiting with fins, masks and snorkels, his bronzed body a human machine of flexed muscles in motion. He looked powerful, brown and masculine.

They strapped on flippers, mask and snorkel and waded backward into the shallows. As soon as the water was deep enough to submerge, Sophie pushed herself off, kicking her way over the beautiful coral formations spread out in pristine clarity beneath them, an underwater garden with masses of darting, brightly-coloured fish.

Coral reefs were essentially living rocks made of colonies of billions of tiny polyps. A miraculous creation and one over which Sophie never ceased to marvel. Drew swam close, guiding, sometimes directing her gaze elsewhere, making Sophie acutely aware of him.

Back on the beach later, Sophie sat on the sand, brushed the water from her face, freed her hair and squeezed out the excess water, ruffling it loose to dry.

Drew hesitated alongside. 'I'm giving scuba lessons to guests later. I'm sure you don't need any tuition but you're welcome to come along and watch.'

She tried to sound composed and unaffected by the nearness of his bare sun-warmed skin. 'Why not.'

After lunch, Sophie made her first preparatory research notes then headed for the instruction pool. Drew and the group had already gathered. Two middle-aged men in good shape, a gorgeous blonde whose bikini left nothing to the imagination, and a freckled, red-haired boy called Marty.

Scuba gear and wetsuits lay on the grass. Drew explained the basics then suggested they all try on their gear. The blonde was not as helpless as she pretended, Sophie suspected, but Drew tactfully helped her.

In turn, each jumped into the pool for their first practise dive, holding their face mask. After the blonde submerged, she thrashed frantically around and resurfaced, spluttering. Drew immediately sprang to her aid and dragged the female from the water. Sophie guessed she wouldn't last long and had probably only signed up to get closer to the instructor!

That evening, Drew didn't appear, so Sophie dined alone.

Afterwards, feeling lost and lonely, she decided on a swim before bed. She changed and made her way to the pool. It was good to slither beneath the surface and feel the cool water caress her skin. She did her usual slow laps then, floating on her back deep in thought, became distracted by a loud splash behind her.

Startled, she rolled over and stood up, her hair streaming in a wet mass.

A head bobbed up beside her. 'Hi, Flipper.' Drew pushed himself up in the water, his impressive body glinting with moisture. 'Like a flight tomorrow?'

Pleasantly surprised by his reappearance, she said, 'I thought Mal had the chopper?'

'He's bringing some tourists out early and the machine will be free for a few hours.'

He shrugged. 'Seems a pity to waste the morning.' When Sophie hesitated, he added, 'We could scout along some beaches.'

Privately, Sophie was ecstatic. She could finally start her work.

Drew baited her hesitation. 'Only if you're interested, of course.'

'You know I am.' She gave him a playful splash.

'See you tomorrow on the beach at eight sharp.' He heaved himself from the water at the side of the pool.

Eight sharp, indeed, she grinned at his back as he disappeared from view along one of the deeply shadowed island pathways. Her research time on the island was shaping up to be exciting. Which she convinced herself had nothing to do with her charming companion.

And no sight or sound of her father

either. Another bonus. Altogether, the immediate future was looking bright.

Chapter 3

Next morning after breakfast, Sophie heard the helicopter return. When she met Drew on the beach as arranged, he stared at her long, slim legs beneath her swimsuit and covering grandpa shirt.

Ignoring her erratic heartbeat, she clamped on a sunhat and sunglasses, and scrambled up into the cockpit beside him. As the chopper lifted off, she could not suppress her excitement. As they flew, she discovered Drew highly knowledgeable about the reefs and turtle-breeding colony locations, exactly what she needed for her work.

They saw dolphins, their sleek bodies leaping and racing through the clear water below them. They skimmed low over nearby island beaches, searching for the green turtles' preferred habitat of shallow water with good growths of sea grass.

Sophie also learned that Drew knew one location where the reptiles were known to regularly migrate to mate and lay their eggs. Sophie knew turtles often returned to the beach where they hatched. They were incubated by the sun's heat and emerged during the night, guided by moonlight toward the waves. So she hoped Drew's local information helped to locate them.

Later in the morning, he headed the chopper towards the crystal clear depths further out where the blue waters streamed across the reef directly beneath them and rollers thundered in from the ocean.

To Sophie's fascination, they landed on a floating helipad anchored in the centre of an atoll's tranquil lagoon. Once outside, she removed her shirt, donned her mask and snorkel, and slipped into the water, immediately transported into undersea enchantment again.

This patch of reef was particularly thick with many species of sea life from the stunning blue and yellow damsel fish to bright blue starfish, and vivid red and white sea slugs.

She explored the new reef and, when she resurfaced, found Drew seated on the pontoon with his feet dangling in the warm waters, a cane basket beside him.

'It's magnificent below,' she breathed, heaving herself up and brushed water from her face and arms.

Drew produced a towel. Gratified by the thoughtful gesture, Sophie accepted with a grateful smile and gave her damp, tangled hair a vigorous rub while he unlatched the hamper crammed with tempting food and poured them each a glass of Chardonnay.

'Food and wine in the middle of the sea.' Sophie chuckled. 'How civilised.' Hungrily, she took a prawn and nibbled its succulent white flesh. 'This has to be heaven.' She tasted her wine.

'Not far off.' Drew demolished a chicken leg and licked his fingers.

Sophie often craved such idyllic dream moments as these in Sydney when she was stuck in traffic or making forced polite conversation during dinner with some snobbish rich heir of J.B.'s choosing, considered an acceptable candidate for a potential merger; business and marriage.

With the effects of the wine and the sun, Sophie sensed she and Drew mellowed toward each other, and an enjoyable, even companionable, silence settled over them.

'You're different today,' he murmured eventually, his gaze drifting across the calm aquamarine ocean around them.

'Am I?' She marvelled at his sensitivity and depth of perception. Few people possessed such a gift. Hoping to keep their friendship strictly business, she suggested, 'Shouldn't we be leaving?'

'If we must,' he taunted with his now familiar and rather charming lopsided grin.

Lethargic and reluctant, they hauled themselves back into the aircraft and headed for Jewel.

In the afternoon, Sophie browsed the island boutique and purchased three more casual outfits to expand her wardrobe. She rarely shopped but enjoyed the spree. It kept her mind occupied and the one low-limit credit card she allowed herself in shape.

Later, torn between reading, another swim or work, she groaned in defeat and forced herself to concentrate on some study texts seated in a deck chair beneath a palm tree overlooking the lagoon pool.

At dusk, with the sun lowered in a huge orange ball to the horizon, Sophie wondered how she could be so pleasurably weary from a helicopter flight, a lazy lunch and an even lazier afternoon.

She squandered another indulgent half hour in a perfumed bath, brushed her glossy chestnut hair until it glowed like silk, then dressed for dinner in her new white strapless sundress splashed with a tropical pattern. She was about to snap out the lights and leave when there was a knock at the door.

Drew's sandy hair ruffled in the evening breeze as he stood before her in linen slacks and a black shirt.

'Dinner again?' He grinned.

Sophie faltered then weakened. Oh, girlfriend or not, what did it matter? They were friends and working companions, nothing more.

'Why not,' she laughed.

He stepped aside to let her pass then escorted her to the restaurant. Resist though she might, Sophie found herself responding to a firm hand on her elbow, a tanned arm gently guiding at her waist, a chair pulled out at the table.

Knowing all the time she probably shouldn't but then common sense would return when she admitted they were dining out in the open, in full view and hardly conducting a clandestine affair.

Sophie rarely noticed Stephanie these days. Perhaps she had time off on the mainland. Her wayward thoughts were interrupted when their drinks arrived and they ordered coral trout from the menu.

Catchy calypso music drifted across from the small band and Sophie unconsciously hummed along. When her eyes settled on Drew, she caught him absorbed in her, staring back.

'Care to dance?' he said in a husky voice.

Sophie wished he hadn't asked because in their present susceptible mood, it might move them into dangerous emotional territory. She couldn't refuse him indefinitely so she accepted with a nod.

His hand sought hers and he led her away. When his arms stole about her, she stiffened with awareness then surrendered and melted against him, giving herself up to the moment. Without a doubt, the music and the man were a dynamic and irresistible combination. It was all too heady and Sophie felt as though she were under a tropical spell.

When Drew's cheek rested against her forehead, the idle thought crossed her mind that he was her perfect height as a dancing partner. When the music ended, they returned to their table for coffee. A short while later, Sophie decided it wiser to leave and rose.

'You don't want to stay for another coffee?' He actually sounded disappointed.

Sophie felt torn. 'No, Drew. I don't think so.'

He pushed his chair back and stood beside her. 'I'll walk with you back then.'

Sophie's heart heaved a deep fateful sight. This was not good. Working together and trying to stay immune from Drew's magnetism was enough of a challenge.

By the time they reached her bungalow porch, Sophie was frantic. The dinner and dancing had been intoxicating and she fumbled distractedly in the dark for her key.

Drew covered her trembling hands with his. 'Sophie?' He tilted her face up to his, drew her into his arms and kissed her until she felt weak all over. All too soon, it ended.

He kissed his finger, placed it gently on her lips and whispered, 'Night, Flipper.'

Stunned by her strong reactions and

emotions for this man, Sophie analysed the edge of suspicion creeping into the corner of her mind. It couldn't be... Not after only two days. Heaven, she couldn't let it happen. He already had another woman. Besides, it would complicate their working relationship. Cool and detached was the solution. Even if she had to beat him off with a pineapple!

It wasn't until she had glided in a euphoric haze into her bungalow that she realised they hadn't arranged when and where to meet tomorrow.

Chapter 4

As it turned out, it didn't matter because Sophie discovered a note stuck to her door when she slipped out early the following morning for her usual swim in the pool.

The *Reef Lady* proved to be a ten metre motor cruiser, white and gleaming. When Sophie first saw it, she was impressed. Drew leapt aboard and offered Sophie his hand. She flinched. Just the touch of his fingers...

She followed him down a short flight of steps into a comfortable saloon. There were windows all around with a galley on one side and a cosy dining alcove on the other. They walked through and Drew opened a polished, wooden door into a cabin.

'I hope you'll find everything you need in here. If you don't, just ask.'

Up on deck, Drew's mouth flickered into a wry grin. 'I know you're anxious to start so if you'd like to untie the bow line for me, we can get underway.'

Sophie liked it that he assumed she was familiar with boats and unfastened the rope. Which of course she was. J.B. had always owned a luxury motor cruiser with its deck spa, pilot and private staff. When she and her siblings had been younger, they had thrilled to the sailing on Sydney harbour among its many secluded half-moon beaches and coves.

They reversed from the pier, cruising at an unhurried leisurely speed away from the island. Sophie stayed on the foredeck enjoying the breeze and the delightful appearance of a school of sociable dolphins cruising before the bow, leaping in great curving arcs from the water. Fascinated, she watched them until they disappeared and Drew brought the *Reef Lady* to anchor in a sheltered sandy lagoon enclosed by a fringe of coral patches.

Anchored over a reef not far from a nearby uninhabited island beach, Sophie noted Drew had their scuba gear checked and ready. They climbed down a ladder to the rear diving platform and plunged in, feet first.

Once underwater, Sophie thought solely as a biologist, fascinated and absorbed by the variety of marine life but always aware of the other human presence beside her. She sensed Drew watching her closely as they kicked themselves along, sea grasses waving in the glassy teal shallows. Sophie gazed up and made out the silhouette of the motor cruiser against the surface above. It was a tranquil world of gently subdued light, unsurpassed beauty and eerie silence, a dreamy, floating environment.

Suddenly, Drew tapped her arm and pointed. Sophie was elated to sight her first green turtle swimming slowly nearby. Covered in thick heavy plate-like scales, its head was too big to be withdrawn into its shell like the tortoise. On land, it used its feet for walking but they became modified into powerful flippers that propelled it through the water. Although naturally awkward on land, the creature was an extremely graceful swimmer and could stay underwater for hours.

She never ceased to marvel that the turtle spent almost its entire life at sea, the females only leaving the sanctuary of water for a short while every second or third year to lay eggs. Sophie mentally noted the location as a potential site to watch for females nesting up on the beach at night.

She felt in harmony with the environment, swimming among the marine life and was disappointed as always when their air tanks were low and time was up. They rose together, surfacing near the boat. Sophie climbed up first, water streaming from her wetsuit.

As they removed their wetsuits, Drew caught her gaze and covered her with a broad smile. 'Success first time down.'

He knew how much it meant to her. Sophie smiled through the salty water trickling from her saturated hair and over her face and nodded.

'I'm looking forward to finding nesting females. That's the main part of my research.'

They took off their scuba gear and wetsuits and Sophie climbed below into the saloon. She poured herself a cool drink before settling into the alcove to scribble notes.

Presently, Drew joined her. He cracked open a can of beer and took a long draught, then pressed a button on the inbuilt stereo.

As he slid into the alcove beside her, soft music filled the saloon and he watched her over the can as he drank.

Distracted, Sophie paused in her writing. His knee brushed hers under the table and, once again, she was irritated that his nearness caused her such deep discomfort. She was here to work. She looked up to find him watching again.

He nodded to her notebook. 'Getting everything down?'

Sophie cleared her throat and lied. 'Yes.'

While he remained close, it was impossible to concentrate. As she bent her head to try again, soft damp strands of her hair fell across the paper. Drew reached out and gently tucked it behind her ear. Strained, Sophie kept writing but the words were little more than a blur on the page.

'Let me know when you're finished. We can head back.'

Sophie sensed an escape. 'I guess I'm mostly done. I can finish later.' Her reply was strained. 'I don't want to hold you up.'

Drew drained his can, leant back against the bench seat and studied her through glinting brown eyes. When he rose, his face was alive with amusement.

'I'll weigh anchor.'

In bare feet and trunks, he leapt the steps from the saloon. Accompanied by a heavy sigh, she crumpled the page she was writing. The cruiser rumbled into life and they headed back, trailing a silver wake across the water, the island a dark mysterious green beneath the later afternoon sun as they approached.

Drew jumped off the boat and secured the rope. His hand grasped Sophie firmly as he assisted her to alight.

She brushed aside a wisp of damp hair. 'Can I help with anything?'

The breeze blew her shirt against the curves of her body and Drew's admiring gaze did not escape her.

'No thanks,' he said, and she felt her face glow rosy from more than the sun.

'I'll see you later then.'

Unable to speak, all Sophie could do was stand weak-kneed on the short pier and watch him walk away.

Back in her bungalow, she channelled her frustration into completing more notes. In her intense preoccupation, she neither noticed nor appreciated the orange blaze of sunset.

It was a hot humid night, typical for this time of year, so Sophie chose a cool outfit for dinner. A brief white top tucked into a silky skirt that flounced around her calves in a swirl of lavender, purple and white.

In the restaurant, Sophie scanned the room for any sign of a familiar face. There wasn't. Soberly, she realised Drew would be with Stephanie. Disappointed, she dined alone, her appetite barely doing justice to the meal. She only picked at her food until she left the restaurant and strolled down to the deserted, moon-washed beach. She kicked off her shoes and leant back against a palm.

Torn with a desperate need to be occupied, she longed for daylight and work. The night was balmy and the moon a pale ball in the velvet sky. She had just decided on a beach ramble before turning in, when she was startled by a familiar deep voice behind her.

'Sophie?'

She spun around, her heart pounding that little bit faster as always in Drew's company. Fortunately, the light refreshing sea air cooled her skin and in the gloom he might not notice. He didn't speak but moved closer. He raised a hand and brushed her silken hair aside, placing an exquisitely light kiss on her neck. Sophie closed her eyes and sighed, longing to give herself up to the feelings welling inside her, but knew she couldn't.

She broke away. 'Don't do this,' she begged. 'You know our relationship is business. It has to be.'

'Why?' he pleaded.

Because I have work to do, she screamed inside, aching, knowing she was attracted to him but could let nothing come of it. She had a Degree to complete, a career to establish and an island to buy. Her eyes silently pleaded with him.

'Give me one good reason.'

'What about Stephanie?'

Drew's eyebrows pulled together in a frown. 'This has nothing to do with her.'

Sophie was shocked. 'Don't you care what she thinks? How she might feel?'

'In certain things,' Drew appeared puzzled. 'But my friendship with you is none of her concern. Why should it be?'

Drew Mitchell really didn't care that he might eventually hurt two women's feelings. For interminable seconds, he contemplated her steady, bewildered gaze.

Finally, he released his hold and said quietly, 'Don't panic, Flipper. I can take a hint. I'm dismissed.'

As Sophie watched him slowly walk away, his hunched, dejected posture almost made her believe she might have hurt his feelings but she couldn't feel guilty or responsible. Integrity and principles were at stake here. Besides, keeping emotional distance from him was paramount and vital to her sanity.

To curb her restlessness that night, she worked on her thesis, finally crawling into bed long after midnight. In the morning, Sophie overslept. When she opened her eyes, the room was already drenched with light and she remembered that, in typically casual Drew Mitchell fashion, no arrangements had been made again and she had no idea where to find him. Sophie didn't know where he went, where he slept. In fact, she knew little about him at all.

She swam, showered and ate breakfast but there was still no sign or message from him. Mid-morning, barefoot, and clad in white shorts and a pink tee shirt tied, she began searching the island only to find Drew annoyingly invisible. Until she learned why.

Not only was the helicopter gone but the *Reef Lady* was missing from her mooring. Sophie had assumed they would be going out in the vessel again today and every day. Puzzled by its absence, she hurried to Reception.

Stephanie beamed at her approach and leaned casually over the desk. 'Good morning.'

'Where's Drew?'

The receptionist was clearly jolted by Sophie's abrupt question. 'He's gone for the day.'

Sophie gaped. 'You're kidding?'

Stephanie shook her head, unaware of the bombshell she had just dropped. 'He left early with a party of Asian tourists.'

Sophie remained silent, stunned in disbelief.

'They arrived late last night,' Stephanie explained. 'They're only staying for the day and wanted to make the most of it. Drew had the only charter boat available so he offered to take them.'

'No message?'

Stephanie shook her head. 'He just asked me to explain and apologise if you were looking for him.'

Sophie exploded. 'But it's okay that I cool my heels and lose valuable time here for a whole day?'

'You couldn't do it in a lovelier place.' Stephanie hinted, endeavouring to smooth over the troubled waters. 'And Drew didn't have time to contact you before he left.' She sent her irate guest an appeasing smile.

'I came here to work. Not relax.' Stephanie eyed Sophie's growing irritation with surprise. 'Well, his attitude is just not good enough.' Sophie thrust her hands roughly into her shorts pockets. 'I'll speak to him when he gets back.' Exasperated, she strode away.

With an entire free day yawning ahead of her, Sophie wisely decided not to wallow. Instead, she slipped on training shoes, patted on her sunhat and made her way down to the water's edge outside her bungalow.

Two children paddled in the shallows and eyed her inquisitively as she fossicked over the reef. Unable to contain their curiosity, they gradually edged closer. The girl nudged the boy and whispered. Sophie grinned to herself and continued exploring.

Eventually, a small female voice said, 'Hello.'

Squatting in the shallows, Sophie looked up into a green-eyed, freckled face shaded from the sun by a multi-coloured peaked sun cap. A pair of pigtails protruded through holes in the top and her face was splotched with bright green sunscreen.

'Hello.' Sophie smiled in return.

The girl bent down with her hands on her knees. 'What are you doing?'

'Searching through the coral.'

'Why?'

A rush of memories flooded back to Sophie. This could have been herself twenty years ago. 'Because I'm a marine biologist and I love anything to do with the sea. Don't you like fossicking around in the water, too?'

'Yes.' The girl beamed. 'We found a crab yesterday.'

'Did you?'

She nodded vigorously. 'In a puddle.'

The boy interrupted, 'You weren't game to pick it up, though. I did,' he added proudly.

'It was only small anyway,' the girl retorted.

'It was probably a soldier crab.' Sophie tactfully intervened.

'How do you know that?' the boy demanded, unconvinced.

'Because I've studied sea creatures for a long time.'

The girls' eyes widened but the boy remained dubious and unimpressed.

Sophie continued paddling with her spectators trailing behind, innocently chattering and asking questions. She pointed out different types of coral, supplied names and explained about them until a woman called out from further along the beach.

'That's our mum,' the girl said. 'We have to go.'

They waved and waded carefully among the coral back to shore. Sophie had enjoyed their company. The children's presence had suppressed her frustration at being neglected by Drew Mitchell all day.

Sophie stopped for lunch, then settled, unwillingly, to read by the pool. Still distracted, she wandered away to a quiet stretch of beach. She had assumed Drew would be at her disposal and available for work every day. Thought she had made it plain but obviously they had misunderstood one another and she hadn't made her requirements clear enough. Unpleasant as it promised to be, she must confront Drew on his return and straighten out their future work arrangements together. If J.B.'s minders found her before she had a chance to do enough research to complete her thesis...

Sophie stretched out in the warm shallows, letting the soothing waters gently wash over her and finally relaxed enough to become engrossed in a novel. The sun, now long past its zenith, gradually lowered and lost its strength, casting fingers of shadow across the beach. The next thing she knew, she was looking at a pair of sandy, brown feet.

'Hi. I see you've passed the time.'

Sophie squinted up at him. 'Not by choice,' she answered testily.

'It was an unexpected booking.'

She tried to re-focus on her book but her attention was caught by his bare toes sinking into the wet sand each time a ripple washed up on the beach around them.

'Stephanie explained,' she said, niggled by his cool indifference and lack of consideration. 'But you could have refused.'

He hunched down beside her. 'You're upset.'

'Of course.' She snapped her book shut. They stood up and faced each other.

'Are you going to let me explain?' His voice lost some of its warmth and patience.

Feeling mutinous but anticipating a decent explanation and apology, Sophie remained wisely silent.

'I know you're angry, but like that rush chopper flight, this trip was unexpected, too. There are private boats and yachts here on the island but Jewel is small for a reason; to keep it intimate and private, and the *Reef Lady* is the only commercial charter available.'

'You're already chartered. By me. I sent you a generous advance.'

Visibly tired and exasperated, Drew's hand raked a path through his hair. 'It was late when Steph called my room, told me about the visitors and their limited time, and made a suggestion. By the time I'd checked the boat and restocked with provisions, it was nearly midnight and I was beat. I checked your bungalow but your light was out and I didn't want to wake you. It was after two when I finally hit my bunk.'

He had made an effort. 'Your attitude is far too casual,' she conceded lightly.

'The pace in tropical Queensland is a little different to Sydney.'

'You've made your point but I don't expect it to happen again. I hired you and I can also fire you.'

Sophie could tell by the hurt in Drew's eyes and the severe set of his mouth that she had stung him, and the instant the unnecessary threat spilled out, she regretted it.

'Your privilege,' Drew said with quiet cool. 'If I'm still your *employee*,' he announced pointedly, 'I'll come by at seven to make plans for tomorrow.'

He turned around and strode back up the beach, leaving Sophie alone and miserable, knowing she had ineptly handled the situation. Not solely from a sense of nagging anxiety to finish her work in case her father sabotaged her efforts, but because of her disturbing attraction to the man she had just reprimanded. Trying to avoid both

Drew and J.B. was equally frustrating and weighed heavily on her mind. Why did life always have to be so complicated?

Chapter 5

Later, after a long bath had soothed Sophie's nerves but before she was fully dressed for dinner, there was a knock at her door. Too early for Drew. He was usually late. She pulled on a robe and answered it, to be greeted by Stephanie, her long tumbling brown hair caught back off her face by a smart red bandana. There was no denying it, the girl was attractive. Drew's interest was understandable.

'Hi.' She smiled. 'Drew's at the watering hole and asked if you could join him there when you're ready.'

He was in the bar already drowning his sorrows and she was expected to come when he snapped his fingers?

Stephanie noticed her frown. 'Everything all right?'

Sophie forced a smile. 'More or less. Why?'

She shrugged. 'Drew's unusually quiet. Is there a problem?'

Sophie took a long breath and admitted, 'We disagreed.'

Stephanie lifted her dark eyebrows. 'I'm surprised. Drew's usually so easy-going.'

'Exactly,' Sophie muttered.

'Because he was away today?' Stephanie probed. Sophie nodded. 'It must have been disappointing for you but he really had no choice.' Stephanie paused. 'Look, I'm probably intruding, but perhaps if I explain his position?'

Sophie shrugged.

'The entire Queensland coast is about tourism. If you neglect potential customers someone else is out there ready to snap them up. It's competitive. You should know that Drew's a businessman, first and last. He's worked hard for over a decade to get established.'

Sophie folded her arms. 'No need to blow his trumpet. I'm aware of his capabilities,' she admitted.

'He takes every job to earn every cent he can get because he has this crazy dream.' Stephanie smiled and grew reflective.

'What is it?'

Stephanie shrugged. 'Ask him some time,' she said with tantalising mischief. 'I'd better get back.'

Arriving at the watering hole ten minutes later, Sophie's blue eyes settled on the trio at the bar. Drew sat on a stool, drink in hand and Stephanie stood beside him, an affectionate arm draped around his shoulder. They listened to the other man, tall like Drew but with thick, blonde hair, olive skin and a dashing smile. Another charmer, Sophie thought, not unkindly.

For an instant, she hesitated, reluctant to intrude and feeling like an outsider. Then, as if they shared a psychic connection, Drew turned and from across the room their gazes locked. His attention didn't waver from Sophie as she approached them, her glossy hair gleaming under the soft lights and her fitted white dress hugging her slender, tanned body. It was as though he challenged her to break the bond.

Realising Drew's attention was diverted, Stephanie followed his gaze. She dropped her arm from his shoulder and smiled.

'Hi, Sophie. Well, I'll be off. I'm at Reception for hours yet.' She kissed Drew on the cheek, said, 'Bye guys,' and left.

The other man slid from his seat and extended a hand to Sophie. 'Mal Beasley. Drew's partner.'

Sophie inclined her head. 'He's mentioned you.'

She sat down on a bar stool, crossed her slim legs and, despite her pounding heart, calmly ordered a cocktail. Drew turned his attention aside and sculled a beer. 'Would you excuse us, Mal? We have some business.'

'Sure.'

Drew missed the other man's wink at Sophie as he moved away.

Bolstered by the light encouragement, Sophie took a deep breath. 'I realise I was curt on the beach earlier but-'

'Yes, you were.'

'And you were selfish.'

He shrugged. 'If you say so. I'm not here to argue,' he said. 'As from tomorrow, I'm at your exclusive disposal until you finish your research.'

Sophie blinked at his abrupt formality.

'I trust the thought pleases you?'

'Naturally. When do we start?'

'Dawn. And bring a change of clothes.'

Sophie was puzzled. 'Why?'

'A precaution. I always go prepared.' Drew drained his beer and stood up. 'Dawn,' he repeated, acknowledged Mal nearby with a departing wave and disappeared into the black gloom of the island gardens.

Mal slid closer around the bar. 'Drew's like a thundercloud lately. Don't know what's got into him. Free for dinner?'

'Love to.' She smiled her acceptance and they found a table.

Sophie discovered Mal an entertaining companion and found herself responding to his jokes and conversation. She liked his uncomplicated friendliness and easy company but, mindful of her early start next day, kept the evening short.

Next morning, as Sophie arrived at the *Reef Lady* clutching a small bag, she felt like an enemy lining up for war. The sleek white vessel lay motionless at anchor over glassy water but there was no sign of her skipper. Sophie clambered aboard and went below. As she dipped her head to enter the galley, Drew looked up.

'Good morning,' she greeted politely, distracted by his denim shorts and bare chest.

He stacked some plates in a cupboard rack and dried his hands on a towel. 'You're early. Good.'

His attitude was cool and, for once, unaccompanied by his trademark heart-stopping smile.

He indicated her bag. 'Stow those away and we can make a start.' He brushed past her and went up on deck.

From the cabin, she heard movement above. As the engine rumbled into life, the boat lurched and she was thrown on to the bunk. She scrambled to her feet in surprise. The skipper was certainly keen this morning! Maybe her words had finally taken effect.

She changed into a swimsuit and climbed above. As the *Reef Lady* ploughed through the calm sea, Sophie moved forward and sat against the rail on the bow, ignoring Drew and enjoying the feel of the invigorating salty mist drifting over her as they cruised along. It might have been a perfect day except for the tension.

Two hours later, they anchored over a reef in offshore shallows and donned their scuba gear. With only the most necessary basic words spoken between them, they tumbled backwards into the water.

Sophie was relieved to be underwater working again, able to regain the peace and solitude of the reef and concentrate on the dive to confirm the location and presence of the turtles they had noticed two days before. Sometimes the turtles emerged on to land to bask in the sun but they were more likely to be found among the marine grasses in the shallows.

After only a short while, she noted a number of the reptiles cruising their undersea world and they spent their remaining air time tracking and observing them until Drew tapped his gauge and they drifted to the surface.

They ate lunch in virtual silence, Drew gazing remotely out to sea while Sophie made more of her endless but necessary notes.

In the afternoon, they dived again. In the saloon afterwards, Sophie resumed her notes but by sunset she grew concerned. Drew had made no attempt to start back for Jewel. Finally, the *Reef Lady* shuddered into life and Sophie sighed with relief. Barely thirty minutes later, the engines died and she heard the grinding of a lowering anchor.

'Something wrong?' she asked when Drew came below.

'No.'

Sophie frowned. 'Then why have we stopped?'

She endured his quiet contemplation before he responded. 'We're not going back.'

'What!' Sophie sprang from her seat.

'You heard.' His face was stony.

Astonished, she said, 'I don't understand. They'll be expecting us.'

'No they won't.'

Exasperated, Sophie finally understood. 'You planned this. They know we're staying out. Why?'

Drew didn't give her an immediate answer, scowling instead. 'For a reason. I'm not sure I've done the right thing.'

'That makes two of us. Feel free to explain.' She crossed her arms over her chest and glared at him.

Drew regarded her steadily for a moment. 'Your father has phoned the island a few times since you arrived. Steph's done her best to be evasive, claiming guest privacy and all that but we're not sure he's convinced.'

Sophie moaned, immediately understanding and forgiving his actions. Sometimes, it seemed all she did was open her mouth just to change feet.

'He was born to make my life difficult.' She grew anxious. 'I have to finish my research.'

'That's why I'm keeping you out here. For tonight at least. You're less accessible.'

With a sigh and half a grin, Sophie said, 'Then I suppose I should thank you for kidnapping me.'

'I can't believe the depths to which your father will sink to interfere in your life.'

'If you knew him, you wouldn't ask. It's called emotional blackmail. Don't worry, I'm wise to it and I refuse to buckle.'

'I admire your grit.'

'He gives me little choice.' With a hopeless shrug, she asked, 'What now?'

'I've got a deck of cards and dominoes,' he waved an arm toward a porthole, 'but there's a whole lot of warm ocean out there. Why not take a midnight swim? It's all yours.'

Sophie shook her head and smiled. How could you not be fascinated by a man who was both irresistible and frustrating at the same time?

'You're not coming?' She suffered the deepest sense of emptiness and disappointment when he shook his head.

'I've got things I want to check here, Flipper. Off you go and enjoy yourself.'

Up on deck, Sophie drew in a deep breath of balmy salt-laden air. The night was still, the ocean calm. They were close to shore and the temptation of the silvered moonlit waters was too strong to resist, so she didn't even try.

She stepped down onto the diving platform at the rear of the boat, for an instant, a slim poised silhouette before diving into the sea.

She stroked out strongly, her body cutting a slender wake that barely rippled the smooth surface. When she reached shallow water, she waded ashore and sat down on the beach. Behind her, there was a bank of low scrub. Nearby she heard the soft rustling of palms and saw their glinting outline against the moon's lemon glow.

She looked back out to the cruiser anchored offshore, tiny specks of light shining out from its cabin. Without fuss or alarm, so she wouldn't be stressed over her father's contact and persistence, Drew had unceremoniously stolen her away so she could finish her thesis in peace and achieve her dream.

Sophie had never confided her outlandish wish to anyone. She didn't know anyone else who had the ludicrous idea to buy an island. Strangely, she sensed there was possibly one person who would understand and in whom she would feel comfortable to confide. And he was out there on that boat. She wondered about *his* dream that Stephanie had mentioned once and decided to ask him when she returned.

Quite simply, he had abducted her to keep J.B. at bay. Drew Mitchell was a man to be admired as much as her father was to be despised for his attempted tyranny.

She had never enjoyed the support of an ally against her father before. Drew Mitchell was no ordinary man. Given different circumstances, she could hold more than ordinary affection for him. But he was already attached and there were things she needed to do before she settled down.

For a long time, Sophie sat on the beach hugging her knees, her toes dug into the soft white sand, the night's balmy warmth caressing her skin. She absorbed the tranquillity and silence, stars twinkling overhead, millions of tiny vapours filling the sky.

Eventually, she sighed and stood up. Best get back. She swam the return distance in a slow and easy crawl, hauling herself aboard the cruiser's low rear platform.

She grinned when she discovered Drew had draped her towel over the side railing. And she had called him thoughtless and selfish today! His attempt to redress the balance perhaps? She dried off, secured the towel about her waist and went below.

Drew greeted her with a mug of cream-topped coffee. She accepted and sipped it gratefully, analysing the taste it left on her tongue, frowning in thought.

'Is this Irish coffee?'

He nodded and joined her in the alcove. She contemplated him. 'Tell me about yourself.'

'Why?'

'You know stuff about me.'

'There's not much to tell.'

'You were born in the Territory and moved here to Queensland ten years ago.

Do you still have family in Darwin?' She gestured for him to continue. 'Over to you.'

'My father was a drunk and died when I was young. My mother worked as a barmaid all her life.' His resentment was controlled, measured.

Sophie agonised over the sadness it must have caused him as a boy. 'No siblings?'

'Just my sister,' he said, as if Sophie should know.

She couldn't resist the opportunity. 'Anyone special in your life?' She held her breath waiting for his reply.

He grinned. 'Who'd want me? I'm too boring. Officially over thirty, single and saving every cent.'

'You sound as ambitious as my father.'

'I plan to be financially secure so I'm never poor again. I help my mother financially as much as I can but she's proud and doing okay. Inheriting my grandfather's boat was the biggest windfall in my life.'

Sophie reserved any comment, stricken with guilt. If only he knew the windfall she was destined to inherit soon! 'Was that the *Reef Lady*?'

Drew shook his head. 'An old cabin

cruiser named the *Constance* after my grandmother. I came to live with her, worked on renovating the boat then advertised her for charters. I had her for five years before I bought the *Reef Lady*.' He paused. 'Tourism has changed. Life's faster pace these days. So I went for my wings and met Mal during flying lessons.' He rinsed their mugs and lounged against the sink as he dried them.

Sophie studied him. Being a Brookfield, she had acquired more than social graces and recognised the same shrewd perception in Drew as in her father.

'You have a strong business instinct.'

'What's life without plans and dreams?'

Sophie seized the opportunity. 'What's yours?'

His gaze sharpened and she almost dissolved beneath his intense dark eyes. He had no idea what power they wielded over her senses. But he remained wary. 'Do you have one?' he countered.

'Yes, as a matter of fact I do.' she readily agreed.

'Swap?'

She nodded, wondering how she would voice and Drew react to her crazy dream.

'Promise but you first though.'

For a moment, he turned charmingly boyish, an engaging habit she had noticed once or twice before. 'I want to live on my own island.'

Sharp as a piece of coral, he watched for her reaction. But he could never have predicted the effect of his announcement.

Sophie grew still and gaped at him, overwhelmed. Feelings rushed through her body and words raced across her mind that she was too stunned to express.

Finally she managed to splutter out, 'No. Way.'

'I know. I'm crazy,' Drew admitted, embarrassed.

Speechless, Sophie kept shaking her head until she finally managed to rasp out in a disbelieving whisper, 'No, no, no. Not at all. This is unbelievable. Too incredible by far.'

She reached out for his hands across the galley table. 'That's exactly what I want. My own island. To live on, research from and preserve the natural habitat.'

'You're having me on.' Drew's voice was filled with doubt even as his dark eyes sparkled with amazement.

'No. I'm serious,' she said with strong conviction, willing him to believe until it seemed he finally did.

Reality dawned and he pulled a wry grin. 'For real?'

'Incredible, isn't it?'

'I'll be damned.' They stared at each other then burst out laughing. 'Wonder who'll make it first?' Drew said.

Sophie inhaled a deep breath and plunged ahead. 'I...um...I'm planning to achieve mine within a year.'

Drew's eyebrows raised with interest. 'J.B. going to buy it for you?' A trace of resentment lay behind his words.

Her smile faded. 'In a way. An inheritance falls due in six months' time on my twenty-fifth birthday.' She gave him a moment to digest the information. He gave a low whistle. 'Money isn't the measure of a person, Drew,' she hurried to explain.

'I know that.'

'And it's only pure luck what family we're born into. Bit like a lottery.' She tried to lighten her news.

'I know.'

In the circumstances, Sophie realised his concession was generous.

'Mum sure could have done with more of the stuff when we were kids growing up without a father. Would have kept some hard times from the back door.'

'I'm sorry you didn't have it easier but money never guarantees happiness. We all learn that soon enough. That's something we must strive for ourselves.'

'I know. Guess I envy your head-start.'

'What I get won't be nearly enough but at least it will be in my bank account. Invested wisely it will grow. I'll get my dream. Eventually.'

Drew studied her. 'What makes you happy, Flipper?'

Oddly, it didn't grate on her nerves when he called her that anymore. 'Blue sky and water,' she replied without hesitation.

'Then we're not so different after all, are we?'

'No, not at all,' she agreed, warmed by his touch and his words, and feeling a new and stronger force spring into life between them. A heady sensation and not a little scary.

Sophie was stirred with a great respect for this man and his quiet determination. He was his own person, happy in his work.

Successful without pressure. Although he might disagree, Sophie noted how unencumbered his life had been compared to hers. And that was exactly how she wanted hers to be in the future.

Before they turned in for the night, each wished the other good luck with their dream.

Snuggled down in her bunk with moonlight gleaming in through her open porthole, Sophie smiled faintly in the dimness at the incredible turn of events the day had brought, sighed and drifted into sleep.

Chapter 6

Next morning when Sophie emerged for breakfast, Drew stood over the galley hotplates and there was already a jug of fruit juice on the table. Any other male that had ever served her a meal worked in a restaurant or in the Brookfield mansion. No way would J.B. ever do anything as personal and thoughtful for her mother. How much more companionable was Drew's easy company. Perhaps the less you had, the more you appreciated its value, and the more you gave and shared.

He turned at her appearance and smiled, 'Morning.'

His dark eyes flickered over her tight white shorts and turquoise shirt as he transferred pancakes on to a plate. 'Sleep well?'

She slid behind the banquette. 'I must have. I don't remember a thing.'

She poured herself some juice and settled to some serious eating, aware that Drew watched her but uncertain why. Maybe he still mulled over the revelation about her inheritance last night. Perhaps she shouldn't have said anything but it had been a relief to confide. Sophie's dream meant everything to her. No way could she ever live the life her father had mapped out.

It was still early when they lifted anchor and cruised back out to the reef, the sea and sky of the new day a brilliant dazzling blue.

Later, they plunged down again into the clear, calm water, enjoying the interplay with the turtles when they found them, carefully following and studying them. As always between dives, Sophie compiled pages of meticulous notes and records.

By late afternoon, the cruiser plied easily through the smooth reef waters back to Jewel. Sophie sat on the rear deck, her face lifted to the sun. Drew called out to gain her attention and beckoned from the fly bridge, so she climbed up to join him.

The wind whipped his hair and he stood, bare feet apart, bronzed hands upon the wheel.

'I have a proposition for you.'

Sophie was intrigued and brushed aside the strands of hair blown across her cheek.

His gaze locked into her alert blue eyes. 'What would you say to spending your second week cruising the coast and islands from Jewel back to Cairns? Give you a chance to research the turtles over a wider area.'

It was an excellent idea and Sophie filled with excitement. When she remained silent in contemplation quickly mulling over the possibilities, he added, 'It would keep us mobile and difficult for your father to reach.'

His persuasive argument caused her to raise a mischievous grin and a chuckle. 'It certainly would.'

'And there will be turtles all along the coast this time of year.'

His case was convincing and enticing but Sophie pondered the obstacles. She wasn't bothered to be alone on the boat with Drew. He had proven himself an ideal guide and host. And despite a couple of light hearted but magnetic passes toward her, mostly a gentleman, too. Especially since Drew saw his advances as minor and harmless.

She had to admit, she would entrust her life to him. Altogether, it was a wonderful opportunity, but what about Stephanie?

'I'll think about it.'

Drew seemed surprised by her hesitation. 'Mal can fly in supplies from Cairns tonight and we could leave first thing in the morning. Could you give me a decision by the time we get back to the island?'

Tempted but unsure, Sophie nodded, and remained deep in thought for the remainder of their return trip.

When they reached Jewel again, the sky was an autumnal blaze and a fiery sun rested on the horizon.

'Made a decision?' Drew asked as he expertly nudged the *Reef Lady* into her mooring.

She certainly had but wasn't at all sure it was the right one. Sophie smiled and crossed her fingers behind her back. 'I'd love to do it.'

'I knew you would,' he teased. 'I'll contact Mal and get preparations underway.'

Drew carried her bag from the boat and, together, they strode along the jetty toward the resort. As Stephanie ran toward them, Sophie's heart sank and she was pierced with a twinge of jealousy to see such happiness on Stephanie's face at Drew's return and that familiar smile of understanding pass between them.

Drew caught and held her hand as they walked to the resort.

'I'm glad you're back early,' Stephanie beamed. 'It's Tropicana Night and I'm off duty.'

Knowing the deep affection between them, Sophie wondered if the other woman would agree to let Drew go off alone on his boat for days with another female. They certainly looked good together and yet Drew treated Stephanie so casually.

She guessed they were just being discreet. A touch here. A word there. Maybe from necessity or agreement since they both worked together on the island.

'Well, I have arrangements to make,' Drew said. 'I'll see you ladies later.' He smiled at them both and disappeared along the bush pathway.

Stephanie turned to Sophie. 'Was your overnight trip successful?' Her huge brown eyes sparkled with mirth.

'Completely,' Sophie replied. 'Seems I should thank you for fielding my father's phone calls. I'm not surprised he traced me here.'

'Glad to help,' Stephanie said. 'See you later,' she called out as she walked away.

By the time Sophie sank into a refreshing bath, her anxiety over her father's attempted control had eased, and she was looking forward to the Tropicana Night.

Since it seemed to be a special celebration, she selected a silky skirt with deep frills in a vivid print of rich blue and gold on white, and topped with a white lace sleeveless blouse. Surveying herself in the mirror, she decided it was suitably festive for the night's tropical theme. She was just preparing to leave when there was a knock on her door.

'It's Stephanie.'

Sophie hesitated. Drew had probably told her of his plans and she hoped the other woman felt comfortable with the idea. 'Come in.'

Stephanie entered, wearing a dress of deep rose that flattered her dark colouring and a halo of frangipani threaded through her glossy, brown hair. Drew would be enchanted, Sophie thought enviously.

'Drew mentioned your trip,' she said cheerfully. 'I think it's a wonderful idea.'

'You do?' Sophie was amazed.

'It should be a great help in your work.'

'You don't mind?'

'No. Why should I?' Stephanie fixed Sophie with a strange stare and half smile. 'My big brother's old enough to do as he wants.'

Sophie gaped. They were siblings? As she recovered from the bombshell, Sophie saw the strong resemblance to Drew in Stephanie's brown eyes and dark complexion. How absurd she hadn't noticed the connection before.

Then she realised their planned research trip was now placed in an entirely new light. Drew didn't have a girlfriend after all. At least, not one she knew about and he hadn't confessed to one when she asked. Had his advances, then, been genuine? Alarmed, Sophie suddenly felt vulnerable to have her emotional safety net removed and her comfort zone invaded.

What to do? Go off alone at sea with a charismatic dreamboat or tell Drew the trip was off and risk her father's intervention? An impossible call. If she postponed this opportunity, who knew when she could get enough time off work to escape up here and finish her thesis again?

Concealing her mixed feelings of joy and dismay, and trying to sound casual, Sophie admitted, 'I didn't realise you were Drew's sister.'

Stephanie arched her well-shaped eyebrows. 'Drew didn't mention it?'

Sophie shook her head. 'No, and your surname is different.'

'Thomas is my married name but I'm separated. My fault,' she explained quickly, noting Sophie's concern. 'Too young.'

'It must have been a difficult time.'

Stephanie shrugged. 'It was at the time but I've never regretted my decision. Although I confess I'm wary to try again. My parents wanted me to return to Darwin but Drew found me a job out here on Jewel. If you're ready, let's walk together.'

Sophie turned out the light and closed the door behind them.

'If I ever do remarry,' Stephanie said, falling into step beside Sophie along the pathway, 'I want stability. Someone hard-working like Drew.' She tossed a mischievous glance at Sophie. 'Now, there's a catch.'

Sophie felt hot beneath Stephanie's teasing scrutiny, smiled but said nothing.

'Often, females come here looking for a holiday romance and he's an obvious target. But he really seems to enjoy spending time with you. Drew would never be interested in anyone who didn't share his interests. You two have a lot in common.'

Something inside Sophie quickened at Stephanie's words. Feeling light hearted at the knowledge, yet privately bewildered, she nervously approached the evening's festivities.

They arrived at the restaurant to find it decorated with coloured lights strung across the ceiling and huge glass bowls of tropical flowers placed around the room, with individual hibiscus blooms on every table. Drew and Mal waited for them and strains of melodic Hawaiian music drifted across the room.

'The wait for you is always worthwhile,' Mal said, lifting Stephanie's fingers to his lips.

Stephanie flushed. 'Put your eyes back

in your head, Beasley, and show us to our table, please,' she chided.

Stephanie and Mal, Sophie thought, for the first time closely observing the couple interacted well. A natural combination. Which rather thrust her and Drew together as a couple for the evening. Sophie found her new awareness of him utterly disturbing.

Drew winked at Sophie and ran an appreciative gaze over her radiant tan and dazzling appearance.

'Hi, Flipper,' he said softly enough for her ears alone.

She blushed, feeling gauche and unsure. All the experience in the world could never have prepared her for his intimate greeting.

He plucked a hibiscus from a nearby table and tucked it behind her ear. His fingers brushed her cheek then fell away. Sophie's stomach tumbled over as he linked hands and followed the others weaving toward a spare table.

The restaurant was crowded, everyone festively dressed and laughing, the music already enticing couples on to the floor. Sophie and Stephanie ordered tropical cocktails and the men drank ice cold beer.

They were enjoying the seafood entree when Mal remarked innocently, 'I believe you two are taking off alone tomorrow.'

Sophie cringed, moving uneasily in her seat at the insinuation. Twenty-four hours earlier, the circumstances would not have bothered her one bit. Now, their situation was reversed.

Tactfully, Drew intervened. 'Yes. Just back to Cairns. It will help Sophie's research,' he said, calm and casual.

Sophie was grateful for his succinct words. A gallant male to the defence of her reputation and Mal's nuance easily dispelled. They chatted until their main course arrived. Afterward, awaiting dessert, the rich strains of a slow Hawaiian melody drifted across to them. Drew didn't even ask. He simply looked across at Sophie who was immediately drawn into the depth of his warm, dark eyes. Instinctively, she rose to dance.

Out on the floor, Drew's broad hand spanned the back of her waist. Even such light pressure was devastating in its effect and she melted into his arms, unable and not wanting to resist. She felt his heartbeat against hers, his silky shirt cool and soft beneath her fingertips.

'Thank you for explaining earlier.'

'Does it bother you that we'll be alone?'

'Of course not,' she responded too swiftly. 'But I guess the trip could be misunderstood.'

'Ah, but we know better, Flipper, don't we?' he mocked, a flicker of mirth twitching his mouth.

Neither could deny nor resist the growing rapport and simmering attraction between them. As if in confirmation, he pulled her closer, pressing his lips against her hair until Sophie gasped at his deliberate enticement. Fighting surrender, she drew back from him, for no other reason than to create physical distance and check her ranging hormones and fluttering heart.

'The Reef is a fascinating place.'

'It's not for everyone.' Drew searched her face with downy soft eyes and grinned. Her unease clearly amused him so he played along. 'But you're a born mermaid, Flipper, aren't you?' he said in a deeply caressing tone.

Sophie wasn't sure she appreciated Drew baiting her this way mere hours before their departure in the morning. She would need to remain on guard against this tantalising heartbreaker. His perception may not have changed but hers certainly had. Dancing was a mistake, too, because Drew used his devilment by drawing her closer again, throwing her senses into overdrive and confusing her anew.

As soon as the music stopped, Sophie escaped back to their table, deliberately diverting her gaze and attention away from Drew as much as possible for the rest of the meal.

When the foursome finally called it a night, Mal and Stephanie left together but Drew lingered. Sophie sighed with tension, feeling safe in a crowd. How on earth would she deal with this man and her emotions in a boat out in the middle of the Coral Sea?

'Come on, Flipper.' Drew slid a possessive arm around her waist. 'You need some sleep.'

Sophie broke free and walked ahead. At her bungalow, she said, 'I thought Mal had to return to Cairns for supplies.'

'He'd already left to return back here to Jewel when I contacted him so I've arranged for a private boat to bring out provisions at daybreak.'

Beneath the intimate arbour outside her door, Drew moved a step closer.

'Drew, I'm not an idle tourist expecting to be romantically entertained,' she warned, placing her hands on his chest to push him away. 'I'm here to work. We can't forget that.'

'Fair enough.' Drew lowered his hands and sank them into his pockets. 'But it doesn't alter the fact that I admire you and find you attractive.'

'Thank you. I'm flattered. But you must promise,' she urged. 'Strictly business.'

'No problem,' he agreed. 'I'm looking forward to being stuck on a boat with you for a week.'

His eyes danced with merriment and Sophie sighed. He was thoroughly enjoying himself at her expense. She wondered if he really appreciated how difficult their situation might become.

Drew moved out into the moonlight, picking a bougainvillaea bloom and twirled it in his fingers. 'Lighten up, Sophie,' he chuckled. 'Everything will work out fine. Leave your bags out here in the morning and I'll take them to the boat.'

He stepped back beneath the archway

toward her. Sophie grew so entranced by his nearness, she almost stopped breathing. She inhaled a sharp, expectant breath but instead of kissing her as she expected and even hoped, he merely trailed the scented flower gently across her cheek. Before she fully recovered her senses, he was walking away, leaving Sophie standing alone in the dark with a hollow sense of disappointment and confusion and loss.

Chapter 7

After a final glance around the bungalow next morning to make sure she had left nothing behind, Sophie walked down to the *Reef Lady*. Drew waited on deck, suntanned and smiling. She held out a hand and he pulled her aboard.

'Now, follow me,' he gestured, 'and I'll show you the radio equipment. You should know how it operates.'

Sophie followed him into the communications cubicle. In the confined space, her body brushed against him and she was shaken by a tremor of weakness. She listened as Drew explained radio procedure and operation for the small radar screen although she was reasonably familiar with the setup from her father's launch.

Soon, the engine shuddered into life and the cruiser edged away from the pier. As Sophie leaned over the side rail, a familiar figure ran down the beach, arms waving madly in farewell. She glanced at Drew, an infectious broad smile plastered across his face and watched him blow a kiss to his sister. Sophie laughed and waved, too. Then their vessel gathered speed and, within fifteen minutes, they lost sight of tiny Jewel cay.

Further out, it was calm and the bow cut a crisp wake as it ploughed through the water. Overwhelmed with bliss, Sophie was engulfed with peace. The clear views, superb royal blue of the sea and wisps of cloud made it look like a picture from a travel brochure.

They dropped anchor in the shallows offshore and made their first dive for the day, gently kicking their way around the reef, searching for the huge reptiles beneath the sea. The pair worked well together, Drew taking photographs to complement Sophie's research.

Afterwards, they continued south so that it was late afternoon when the radio crackled into life. Checking her scuba gear, Sophie didn't take any notice until Drew emerged on deck.

'Does the name Brookfield ring a bell?'

Sophie groaned. 'J.B?'

Drew nodded. 'He's on Jewel. He must have pressured Stephanie.'

Why wasn't she surprised Sophie wondered? Knowing her father's domination, her annoyance simmered. How dare he intrude like this? He had no right nor place in her life out here.

'I better see what he wants,' she sighed and reluctantly moved past Drew to go below.

At the radio console, Sophie pressed the transmitter. '*Reef Lady* to Jewel, over.'

'Where are you?' her father snapped in reply.

'Out on the reef, over.'

No way would she reveal their location. Let him search by plane to find her if he dared and it was so important to interfere in her life. Although her instincts told her he might not push quite as far as kidnapping at sea. She marvelled at the disruption to his life it must have caused to pursue her up here. She almost felt sorry for her father's desperation, trying to get her back, and might have felt flattered except she knew his motives were entirely selfish. Even if she had wanted to be persuaded, which she didn't, forceful domination was no way to achieve it.

'When are you returning to the island?'

Sophie glanced at Drew lounging against the doorway, and gripped the transmitter tighter, her knuckles white. 'I'm not, over.'

Her abrupt reply apparently floored him because the crackling line went dead for a long moment before scratching into life again.

'You must, Sophie. Turn back now. My time is valuable.'

And hers wasn't? 'No can do. I'll be back in a week, over.'

'You'll regret this young lady.'

Never. She trembled and sighed over the anger in his voice, not deeming his threat worthy of a response.

This time, the transmitter stayed silent.

'He flew all the way up here to try and stop you?' Drew said quietly in disbelief.

Sophie shrugged, linking her hands together to stop them shaking. 'He built the company from nothing. He's a self-made millionaire. He wants one of his children to take it over. It means everything to him.'

'More than his family?'

Sophie's mouth twisted in irony. 'Probably. The irony is, he's created such a successful monster of responsibility, you would have to sacrifice your whole life to manage it.'

Drew laid a hand over hers in understanding. 'You okay?'

She nodded.

'Then let's get back to work.'

Toward evening, they anchored in a sheltered lagoon. While Drew prepared dinner, Sophie tried vainly to re-establish her writing mood after losing concentration since her father's unsettling contact. Hopefully, he had returned to Sydney but she didn't doubt he was already devising some other means of sabotaging her independence.

Giving up in frustration, she wandered up on deck to find Drew wrapping steaks and potatoes in foil. 'Can I help?'

'You sure can. We're having a barbeque so you could search for driftwood on the beach when we wade ashore if you like?'

She nodded. He packed utensils and supplies in a bag and tossed it over his shoulder. Sophie followed and found kindling while Drew set up for the meal and then built a fire. Sitting on the sand hugging her knees, she watched the flames grow and the dry wood spitting sparks into the twilight, conscious of the isolation alone by a campfire on an uninhabited island. The peace and wonder of it all settled her anxiety since her father's radio contact.

Drew buried the potatoes to bake in the glowing coals and set steaks to sizzle on a portable grill. The meaty aroma raised Sophie's appetite. She watched Drew's pensive face in the firelight as he turned the meat. Preoccupied with the complete contrast between Drew and her father, Sophie retreated into thought. When the meat was cooked, Drew sliced open the steaming potatoes and smothered them with butter, then filled two wine glasses and nestled the stems to anchor them in the sand.

They ate in silence, absorbing the brilliant orange sunset. When they had finished, with the depleted warmth from the fire and a fresh wind blowing in off the water, Sophie shivered.

Drew noticed and moved closer, placing a windcheater about her shoulders. 'It's getting cool. We should go back to the boat.'

'Yes.' She stared into the dying coals, wishing he had kept his arm around her but knowing it was wise that he didn't.

In the dimness, he sought her fingers and pulled her up beside him. She brushed sand from the seat of her shorts and, with the most casual glance she could muster under the circumstances, managed to say, 'The meal was lovely. Thank you.'

Long before, the moon had risen and now cast a shimmering band across the water.

In the silver light, Drew's eyes assumed a gentle yearning. 'You go ahead,' he said in a husky voice. 'You have work to do. I'll clean up here then come and make coffee.'

Was he keeping them apart for safety? Sophie hugged the windcheater tighter against the chill and waded back to the boat, staying in her cabin making notes. Much later, she heard Drew return and movement in the galley, then a tap on her door.

'Come in.'

Drew entered, trails of steam and the rich aroma of coffee rising from the mugs he carried. He set one down beside her. Sophie expected him to leave but he perched on her bunk. Trying to ignore him, she turned back to her writing.

'Do you have much to do?'

She nodded, aware she was being unsociable but needing to create distance whenever he was around.

'I'll leave you alone, then.'

She heard the bunk creak as Drew rose to leave, his voice holding a softness that made her feel guilty for sounding unkind. If she was to survive another six days, it was vital!

'We'll dive at first light.'

'Great.'

The door shut behind him. Annoyed that his electric presence had left her deeply shaken, Sophie forced herself to move the pen over the pages again. By eleven, she was exhausted but pleased with her efforts and longed for a breath of fresh air. She listened and, when nothing stirred, crept up on deck. The moment she stepped out into the moonlight, she noticed him, leaning over the railing.

Because she had stumbled on the last step and stubbed her toe, she said, 'Ouch!'

Drew turned at her approach.

'I didn't mean to interrupt you,' she apologised, rubbing her foot then hobbling closer.

'You'll always disturb me, Flipper.'

Sophie was deeply aware that his gaze ran over her fitted slacks and pink knit top that softly followed the dips and curves of her body. A fresh breeze blew across the deck and lifted her free hair in a silky veil across her cheek. She noticed an agonising look in Drew's eyes before he turned and looked away out over the sea.

'I like to come up here at night. Drains the mind and soul of cares,' he said absently.

'I didn't think you had any cares.'

'I care about *you*, Sophie.' For a moment, it seemed as though the world had stopped and her heart skipped a beat, until he added, 'And every passenger who's my responsibility. Your life and safety are in my hands.'

As always, Sophie found the strain of just being near him like pleasurable yet unbearable pain, and wished she had not come.

'Finished work for the night?' Drew broke the discomfort.

She nodded. Their conversation was stilted but safe.

'Why is your work so important to you,

Sophie? I know you're conscientious about your thesis and keen to do well so you can become independent, but I sense there's more.'

Some people were born with the gift of perception and intuition. Drew Mitchell, it seemed, was one of them. Because a trusting friendship, mutual respect and easy camaraderie had blossomed between them over recent days, Sophie felt she could confide in him.

'Obviously my father wants me to join him.' Sophie pulled a wry grin. 'His tactics speak for themselves. But you don't know why.'

Drew frowned. 'I had wondered. Go on,' he prompted quietly beside her.

Sophie turned her gaze out over the dark velvety sea, growing wistful and a little sad.

'I had two brothers. Richard was the oldest. Father's heir and favoured child. And David.' Sophie paused. 'Richard was everything J.B. wanted him to be. Smart, ambitious and groomed to succeed.' She swallowed against the bittersweet memories of a tragedy that had split their family apart.

'Five years ago, there was a boating accident at our holiday house at Palm Beach, north of Sydney. No one's fault really. The boys were skylarking too far out. A freak wave caught them unaware and overturned their small rowboat. David managed to swim ashore but Richard drowned.' Sophie pushed back the memory and its accompanying pain.

Sensitive to her distress, Drew reached across and squeezed her hand in comfort. 'Mother was inconsolable,' she went on. 'Father was shattered, too, of course, but in a different way. All he saw was his shining light extinguished and the company's future management threatened. He blamed David and loaded him with guilt to make him feel a sense of duty, an obligation to join the company in Richard's place. But Davy's an outdoor person like me. He'd shrivel up behind a desk on the fiftieth floor of a city skyscraper. And J.B. knew it. In the end, my brother couldn't take any more and left. Became a drifter, a nomad, and is probably never destined to find roots until he finds peace within himself. We rarely hear from him. He's somewhere out there in the world.' Her gaze drifted across the moonlit ocean.

'Which leaves you.'

Sophie nodded and her tone, previously softened with memories, grew terse. 'The sad bottom line is Father only cares about the company and making money, not the lives or feelings of his family. I don't want any part of his world. For the last four years, I've worked and studied to get away. I've seen what hunger for power and material possessions can do.'

She shook her head. 'It's all so false. It's not who I am or where I want to be. So yes,' she admitted, half turning to Drew, 'I take my study seriously because I have a plan, a crazy ambition like you to be on my own island where I can live and work in peace and harmony with nature to preserve it and bring less fortunate children there for holidays. To give them an appreciation of our planet and an opportunity they might otherwise never have. To let them know you don't need money to get somewhere in life or make a difference. You just need a passion.'

'You're an incredible woman, Sophie Brookfield,' Drew murmured, placing an arm about her shoulder and gently caressing her arm until she could barely breathe.

Spellbound, she turned to him. His head

lowered toward hers until their lips were only inches apart. Vulnerable, Sophie succumbed. Drew's salty lips met hers in a long and tender kiss that sent thrills of pleasure along her spine. Nurtured by the strength and warmth of his body against hers, she willingly sank into the embrace.

Sophie had promised herself she would be wary, avoid this scenario but now the moment had arrived she found herself overcome by deep and tender emotions she had never experienced before. Feelings so overwhelming they beckoned her with such yearning against her will, she was helpless to resist. When Drew's stirring kiss finally ended, Sophie opened her eyes. His mouth hovered over her face, his raking gaze raw with hunger.

'Sophie, I want you in my life,' he whispered.

She swallowed. That could mean anything. For a while. Forever. She dared not ask. She forced herself to be realistic. She would give her love to Drew in a heartbeat but knew if she did, there was no turning back. At least for her. Any commitment she made would be given once and for all time. In bittersweet agony, she sensed in her heart that it was not the right time for either of them.

'Drew-'

He pressed a finger gently over her lips. 'One day. Maybe?'

Sophie's brow creased with pain that his interpretation of their love did not equal hers. A crushing pity for they shared something extremely special. When she returned to Sydney, he would remember her fondly with a smile but go on to meet someone else. At that thought, she stiffened and pulled away, mustering every grain of willpower she possessed.

'If it's meant to be,' Sophie conceded, then slowly turned and went below to the safety of her cabin, running from Drew and reality and the arms she wanted around her. She accepted the deep and genuine longing for him, no matter how hard it was to bear, but he hadn't mentioned love and it seemed too early and presumptuous to expect it.

Next morning, Sophie's eyes fluttered open to another warm and magical tropical morning. For a moment, she lay indulgently on her bunk. There was a familiar whistling, movement in the galley, the aroma of coffee. Reluctantly, she forced herself to rise and face Drew again.

He reacted as though their explosive kiss last night had never happened and eyed her casually. Or did he just conceal his emotions better than she? What was really flashing through that quick mind?

He paused, slicing mango. 'Are you all right?'

'Why shouldn't I be?' she said defensively.

'Our kiss.'

'It was...good,' she hedged.

Drew scoffed. 'Good! It was volcanic.'

So, he felt more than he admitted at the time. He was right, of course, but she would never allow herself to show it and make a fool of herself unless Drew conceded more.

'It was just a memorable kiss, Drew. Let's put it down to a moonlit night and move on, okay?'

'You're a challenge, Sophie Brookfield,' he said warmly.

Is that all he thought of her? A possible conquest? In his dreams! Sophie smarted at this apparent indifference and casually began breakfast, pretending she didn't care. After toast and coffee, Drew spread out a chart on the table and tactfully eased into a discussion of the day's plans.

They headed further along the coast until they found breeding turtles and anchored for the day. In the days that followed, cruising the tranquil waters among lush green islands, Sophie was aware of a marked change taking place within her. Alarmingly strong and dangerous feelings she recognised as love. Madness, and breaking all the rules, when Drew considered her little more than a light hearted romance. She had fallen big time and regretted her lack of self-control in letting her emotions get out of hand. She adored Drew whereas he gave the impression he was just out for fun.

Always, on the boat or underwater, Sophie constantly felt Drew's eyes on her. It could have been concern for her safety but feminine intuition told her he would not refuse a casual fling. To deter him, she tied her hair back, plain and severe, and covered her bathing suit with one of her huge floppy shirts. As well, as much as possible on a confined boat, she kept her distance but Drew remained watchful of her every move.

They dived every day until Sophie had amassed a thorough collection of data, and

Drew had taken endless photographs to complement her research.

On the fourth morning, as Sophie fished for their midday lunch from the aft diving platform, their attraction was unwittingly sharpened. Excitedly reeling in her catch, she teetered over the edge of the boat railing. Without hesitation, Drew leapt to her rescue.

Held safely and steadied in his strong tanned arms, Sophie successfully landed a red coral trout, flapping on deck. In her delight and preoccupation, for once Sophie ignored his nearness until their eyes met and her laughter faded.

Afraid he might kiss her again and dissolve her good intentions, she warned him lightly, 'Don't even think about it, Mitchell. You'll spoil a perfectly good friendship.' Who was she kidding, she groaned to herself?

'You're lucky I've been able to keep my hands off you so far, Flipper,' he growled with poor humour.

He removed the hook from the fish's mouth and scaled her catch for lunch.

That afternoon, they sighted an island national park covered with thick forest, rising wild and magnificent from the sea, its peaks much higher than the cays, separated from the mainland by a deep channel.

Drew dropped anchor. 'Let's get to work, Flipper. If you like, I'll let you skipper the *Reef Lady* later.'

'Could I?' Her eyes sparkled as she adjusted her air tank. She had never been allowed on her father's boat since it was always captained.

Drew flashed her a winning smile. 'If you behave yourself.'

She pulled a face and ignored his jibe. Moments later, they broke the surface of the placid lagoon and tumbled into the sea, descending once more into the beautiful and fascinating submarine world.

True to his word, Drew beckoned to Sophie when they were underway on the boat again. She patted on her straw hat and joined Drew on the fly bridge. Following his instruction, she steered the cruiser from the shallows, exhilarated by the thrill of controlling the powerful boat.

'Increase your speed.' He stood beside her. 'And keep her steady on this bearing, okay?'

The vista about them was serene and

indescribably beautiful. The forested emerald mountains sweeping upward from the sea, the smoothness of the water only disturbed by the rolling silver trail the cruiser left behind. It was impossible to believe they were not in their own very special world.

Toward sunset, they anchored for the night. For dinner, Sophie changed into a sarong of blue and gold, leaving her feet bare. Catching sight of Drew in the galley before he turned, Sophie yearned for him to return her feelings. He was so incredibly attractive in his unbuttoned tropical shirt, with a hand towel slung over one shoulder. She longed to go up and ruffle his hair or fling her arms around him in playful affection.

The instant he sensed movement, Drew swung to face her. Sophie rubbed her arms, trying to feel unaffected by the tenderness in his eyes.

'Dinner won't be long. Care for a drink?'

She shook her head and escaped up on deck. A tranquil seascape greeted her, softly washed by a three-quarter moon and the first scattering of stars in the velvet sky. Her research and time with Drew was ending. Soon, they would part and go their separate ways. She heaved a despondent sigh.

Presently, Drew joined her. 'Tomorrow's our last full day together. I'm going to miss all this. I've enjoyed our friendship.'

He leaned across and kissed her playfully on the nose. Friendship! She died inside. He felt nothing more? Her misery was complete.

'Come on.' He caught her hand. 'I've cooked lobster.'

'My favourite.' She forced a smile. The sooner they parted, the better.

Chapter 8

After a swim and breakfast next morning, they rambled along the deserted island beach together, their footprints the only impressions in the unmarked sand. Even through her sadness, Sophie was entranced. She had never seen such unspoiled beauty. She dreaded the thought of leaving Drew, finding it impossible to concentrate all day. Their last dive was purely for pleasure.

Afterwards, while Drew washed his camera equipment for the last time, Sophie showered and changed. When she emerged, he was in the galley preparing a seafood salad of coral trout and lobster he had caught during the day.

'Are you sure I can't help?'

A strange tone entered his voice. 'I've grown accustomed to looking after you.'

Her throat went dry and her eyes stung with tears she refused to let fall.

'I'm going to climb to the top of that hill.' She indicated a low promontory above the beach.

'Take care.' He caught her hand as she left. She forced herself to look up and give him an unsteady smile, letting her fingers drop away. Sometimes she almost felt... But no, it was surely all in her imagination.

She clambered from the boat and waded ashore, scrambling barefoot over grass, rocks and low scrub to the summit. Panting, she turned around and let the wind stream back the hair from her face. Inhaling deeply, Sophie savoured the ocean glinting in the sunset.

She sat down, hugging her knees, imploring her body to absorb the evening calm and still her torment. In a small way, by its simplicity, the magic serenity of the coming night partially eased her heart's burden. Why had she let it happen? Allow herself to fall in love and not have it returned? It was so one sided and lonely.

As darkness fell, she saw Drew beckon to her from the boat far below. Sophie sighed. He had become so much a part of her. She stood up and raised an arm to acknowledge that she had seen him. Then she noticed that he was continuing to wave madly and pointing toward the beach. Sophie frowned as she picked her way downhill, at the same time trying to follow the direction Drew had indicated and discover the reason.

Then she saw it.

A large female green turtle slowly dragging herself up the beach not far from the boat. They heavy burden of its body and flippers left a wide marked trail in the damp sand as it crawled.

Sophie filled with excitement and pushed her footsteps faster in descent. She knew the green turtle spent most of its life at sea, only the female leaving the sanctuary of water for a short time every second or third year to lay its eggs. So this was a potentially very special event. What a thrill to be in the exact location where it was about to happen. And what a treasured finale to complete research for her thesis.

When she reached the bottom of the hill, Sophie sped across the sand and waded through the shallows back to the boat. She chided her own haste, knowing the entire turtle egg-laying process would take hours.

Drew waited aft, beaming, and lent her

a hand to climb up onto the diving platform.

'What about dinner?' she asked when she reached him.

'It can wait. Unless you're starving again,' he teased.

'No,' she replied hastily, not wanting to miss anything. 'I'll just change into more practical clothing.'

Sophie noticed Drew was already wearing casual beach trousers and a tee shirt with his camera gear and a large flashlight gathered together nearby. In her cabin, Sophie quickly slipped on light slacks and grabbed a windbreaker before reappearing on deck to join Drew.

During her short absence, he had placed all of his gear into a backpack.

'Ready?'

She nodded, they rolled up their trousers and waded ashore. Meanwhile, the turtle had struggled farther up the beach and begun the arduous task of excavating a large depression by removing sand with her front flippers.

Sophie sprawled out on her stomach on the sand nearby, propping her chin in her hands, and watched, enthralled. Drew settled beside her, switched on the light and began to capture the special event on film.

'I've never seen this before,' she whispered. 'I guess you have though.'

Drew nodded. 'A few times but it never loses its magic.'

Sophie felt humbled to observe the huge lumbering reptile at all, let alone so closely with a dress circle view. She sighed as she witnessed one of nature's miracles. The turtle seemed completely unperturbed by their presence.

Feeling stiff, Sophie re-settled into a more comfortable position. After what seemed ages, the remarkable moment arrived when the mother began to lay the first of her eggs. Sophie glanced at Drew who had temporarily stopped taking photographs in awe of the event.

'Technically, I know it isn't, but you feel like you're witnessing a mother giving birth, don't you?' he said.

Sophie nodded. 'Exactly. And she'll lay several more batches over the next few weeks. She'll be exhausted.'

'No wonder she doesn't reproduce every year,' Drew quipped with a chuckle.

'And they're all the more precious because of the hundreds she lays, only a few will survive their first year.'

'I often think there's nothing nobler than the job of motherhood,' Drew said quietly.

He would never cease to surprise her, Sophie decided. With a tug of her heart, she warmed to him even more when she knew she shouldn't. After a while, the turtle pushed the sand back over the eggs and began the slow process of hauling herself toward the sea.

As they stood up and brushed the sand from their clothes, Sophie felt a keen sense of nostalgic loss that in a few months, the tiny vulnerable turtle hatchlings would never see their mother. They would dig their way to the sand's surface at night and scuttle madly for the sea.

'Wonderful,' Sophie breathed. 'I won't ever forget tonight.' Not only for the experience but because Drew had shared it with her. He loaded his backpack and reached for her hand.

'Come on, Flipper. Let's go and eat.'

Fingers entwined, they sauntered toward the water and the boat. Aboard the *Reef Lady* again, Sophie freshened up, then slid into the dining banquette beside Drew as he poured them each a glass of wine to accompany their seafood.

He raised his drink in a toast. 'To you.'

Their eyes met over the glasses and a charged break settled between them. Speechless, Sophie hoped he wasn't going to make a soppy speech or she would grow tearful. She didn't think she could bear too many sentiments.

But instead, he asked, 'What are your plans when you get back to Sydney?'

Sophie filled with relief at the respite. 'Finish university, find a job and buy an island. In that order. What about you?' She kept her gaze lowered and picked at her food.

'More charters. Save. Buy an island. In that order.'

When she finally braved a glance at him, they shared an understanding grin. Sophie privately winced. It was so difficult being so close to this man, showered by his devastating smile and trying to remain unaffected.

Clearly, his feelings remained platonic whereas she, foolish woman, had fallen head over heels in love. She swallowed against the emotions building inside her. She may only have known Drew for two weeks but there was absolutely no doubt or question in her heart and mind - he was the man she loved.

Next morning at dawn, Sophie lay in her bunk and stared at the cabin roof. Their last hours together! She forced herself from the bunk and into the shower cubicle before carelessly tossing her clothes into her case ready for the journey ashore and her flight back to Sydney. She slipped on a blue linen dress with a wide antique belt, glitzy leather sandals and then braved facing Drew.

In the galley, they regarded each other warily, her skipper dressed in his official white uniform, looking as handsome and virile as the first time she had set eyes on him only two weeks before. Irrationally, Sophie longed to be in the comfort of his arms.

'You're looking smart this morning.'

'Back to civilisation,' she murmured awkwardly.

She barely touched her food and was grateful when Drew said, 'Ready to leave?' an unusual edge to his voice.

Of course she wasn't, but Sophie nodded anyway and purposely stayed below deck during their last short journey into Cairns. The less she saw of Drew, the less it hurt. She suddenly felt as if a thundercloud had gathered overhead, spoiling the brilliant Queensland day and she struggled helplessly with her crumbling emotions.

After two idyllic weeks, reality had finally returned. Drew guided the *Reef Lady* into Trinity Inlet and steered her to their berth in the marina among other yachts and boats gleaming white on the blue water against a backdrop of green tropical mountains.

From her reading, Sophie knew the port had been first settled well over a century before to serve miners working in nearby goldfields and, during the Second World War, a flying boat base had been located here. Inland lay a patchwork countryside of green squares, dairy farms and sugar cane fields.

Today however, distracted, Sophie was incapable of rational thought to appreciate her tropical surroundings. She stepped ashore onto the boardwalk as Drew unloaded her luggage, appearing calm and unperturbed by her imminent departure.

To her surprise, he checked his watch

and said, 'We have time for a quick tour before your flight.' He strode off toward the car park.

Forced to follow, Sophie ran to keep up with his purposeful, long-legged strides. He was right but she had hoped he would simply drop her off and leave.

'Tour of what?'

'You'll see.'

Sophie gasped in irritation. 'Now?'

'That's right.'

Sophie was indignant. He was being hurtful. It was unfair to delay their parting. But then, she remembered, he obviously wasn't suffering as she did so he wouldn't notice or care.

He loaded her cases into the rear of a red hatchback and, fixing a tenacious hold on her elbow, steered her around to the passenger door. As he held it open, she flashed him a dark look and shook her arm free. Unwillingly, she climbed in and he slid behind the wheel.

He drove into the city and parked the car. It seemed pointless wandering through the older parts of the city and around the harbour area, along the Esplanade and wharf streets. But Sophie forced herself to persevere as they passed by the many old buildings with their wide verandas that provided welcome shade from the hot morning sun.

Acting off-hand and casual, Drew bought her an ice cream. When they finally returned to the car, Sophie breathed a sigh of relief that at last they would head for the airport. But again he amazed her and headed west in the opposite direction toward the foothills.

'Where are we going now?' she demanded.

'To visit Constance,' he informed her evenly, keeping his gaze on the road ahead.

'Your grandmother? Why?'

'I haven't visited her for a while. You'll enjoy meeting her.'

'I would have preferred to be asked first.' And because it seemed pointless in light of the fact that they would never see each other again.

Annoyed by his presumption, Sophie endured the drive in silence. Like many dwellings in the tropics, the house they approached was elevated on stilts and surrounded by a latticed veranda, with lush tropical pot plants underneath.

As they pulled up and alighted, a thin woman in a floral dress appeared on the veranda above them. She leaned on a walking stick and, at the sight of visitors, her lined face beamed.

'My handsome grandson,' she exclaimed in a soft, high voice and then scolded, 'where have you been for the last month?'

Drew took the steps two at a time and hugged her. 'If I came back too often, you wouldn't miss me.'

'Well, who's your friend then?' she demanded kindly.

The woman eyed Sophie who had deliberately held back, not wishing to intrude on their greeting. She climbed up the steps and Drew gently moved aside.

'Grandmother, this is Sophie Brookfield.'

Her bony, wrinkled fingers grasped and patted Sophie's hand. 'Nice to meet you, dear.'

'How do you do, Mrs Mitchell.'

'Constance. Mrs Mitchell makes me sound old.' Shrewd, sparkling eyes absorbed Sophie completely. 'What pretty hair you have, dear.' She glanced at Drew. 'I suppose you can't stay, as usual.'

Drew shrugged. 'Sophie's leaving and I have another cruise to organise.'

Just like that. So flippant, Sophie thought in dismay as though her leaving didn't matter to him. Whereas she felt burdened with a deep ache at her loss.

Constance shook her head ruefully. 'You young people live too fast. Rushing here, rushing there. You ought to slow down a bit,' she gently chastised. 'Come along inside. You're not leaving until I've made a pot of tea.' She cast a disapproving glance at her grandson. 'I suppose you still drink that dreadful coffee?'

Drew stepped forward, grinning, and opened the front door for his grandmother. 'And I'll bet you still keep a jar in the pantry especially for me.'

She scoffed good-naturedly, then disappeared down the wide passage. Sophie preceded Drew into a pleasantly cluttered but airy sunroom where a large ceiling fan hummed overhead.

She sank into a comfortable padded cane chair and gracefully crossed her legs at the ankles. Drew sat opposite on a well-worn sofa, his amused eyes hovering over her.

Evading his gaze, Sophie allowed her

attention to drift around the room. She recognised a younger, smiling Drew in a photograph, holding up a large fish beside an elderly man who had an arm around his shoulder. Sophie noticed a younger image of the same man in a sepia wedding portrait with Constance and assumed it was Drew's grandfather.

Apart from the ticking of a clock and a kettle whistling in the background, the room was hushed. Sophie shifted uncomfortably in the strained atmosphere since Drew made no attempt to talk, and she was relieved when Constance returned. The spritely woman gave Drew his mug of coffee then poured two cups of tea from a silver pot.

Handing one to Sophie, she said abruptly, 'So, you two have become friends?'

Drew glanced at Sophie, catching the rosy colour burning a path across her cheeks. She wondered how he intended to respond.

'I'd like to think so. I hope Sophie agrees.'

She smiled to conceal her pain and nodded.

'Drew's never brought a young woman to visit before.' She paused, studying her guest. 'Probably thought they'd be scared away at the sight of an old prune like me.'

Drew crossed one leg easily over the other and sipped his coffee, ignoring his grandmother with a private grin.

'And what is your father's line of work, Sophie?' Constance asked, offering her a plate of biscuits and fruit cake.

She accepted a biscuit. 'He runs a family company in Sydney.'

Drew raised his eyebrows, obviously surprised by her vast understatement.

'That's the best way.' She wrinkled her nose. 'Be your own boss. Drew has the right idea there, too.'

'I didn't have any choice,' Drew teased good-naturedly. 'The Old Man left me the *Constance*.'

'Go on, with you,' she scoffed, 'you'd be thoroughly bored if you had to spend more than a few days on dry land. You loved every minute you spent at sea with your grandfather.' She faced Sophie. 'What do you do, dear?'

'I'm a marine biologist. At least, I will be soon when I'm qualified.'

Constance raised surprised grey eyebrows. 'Rather an important occupation for a woman, isn't it?'

A smile tugged at the corners of Sophie's mouth. How could she take offence, for the comment was made with lively interest?

'Not really. I've always loved the water. That's how I met Drew. I chartered his boat for green turtle research for my university thesis.'

'Green turtles. My goodness.' The woman's mischievous eyes lit up. 'Well, you two would make a good team then, wouldn't you?'

Drew gave a helpless shrug, leaving Sophie to field the awkward comment alone. Sophie decided no comment was safest and remained silent. To her relief, the subject changed and the conversation veered onto safer waters but when a mantle clock chimed one, she grew edgy, impatient to make her flight, having no idea why Drew had brought her out here.

His grandmother was charming but she flashed an appealing glance at Drew. 'My flight leaves in fifty minutes.'

Drew took her tactful hint and they rose

to leave.

As they walked on to the breezy veranda moments later, Mrs Mitchell chastised her grandson. 'Your hardly stay here anymore.'

'Soon.' He kissed her on the forehead. 'Promise.'

'How's your sister? Has she divorced that useless young man yet?'

Drew grinned. 'Steph's due for leave soon. I'm sure she'll come and see you.'

'For longer than you, I hope.'

As they departed, Sophie thought Drew's grandmother settled a particularly fond look over her considering they had just met. But she seemed a dear and friendly old thing. Sophie could understand Drew's fondness for her.

Minus conversation as they sped toward the airport, Sophie felt aggravated because Drew had deliberately prolonged the agony of departure. Worse, she had to suffer the crushing knowledge that he wasn't in the least bothered about her leaving.

Inside the terminal building, unable to settle before her three-hour flight home, Sophie wandered and paced.

'You needn't wait,' she told Drew,

dreading their goodbye. 'I'll be fine.'

He looked so gorgeous and unconcerned, whereas she felt utterly wretched. Though she supposed it was courteous of him to wait for her, it merely made their parting all the more difficult. When Sophie's flight was called, Drew remained calmly enigmatic, hands sunk into his uniform pockets. Sophie envied his composure but felt a surge of pride that he looked so stunning and was the man at her side seeing her off.

'That's me,' Sophie smiled weakly, struggling for composure.

She could barely look at him and although touching would be a mistake, she longed for even the slightest physical contact.

'You should receive the photographs I took in about a week,' Drew said.

Sophie swallowed hard, forcing herself to remain detached. 'I look forward to seeing them.'

'Good luck, Sophie.' He imposed a long, searching look over her stricken face.

'Goodbye, Drew. Thanks for everything.'

Though she fought against them, she

felt tears forming in her eyes and panicked lest she became weepy. They were actually parting. He was really letting her go! Sophie imagined a flash of pain across Drew's eyes and, for a moment, believed that he actually felt even a little regret at her departure but knew it was impossible. He could never feel as wretched as she did at this moment. She was crushed to be so heartlessly rejected. Why didn't he press her to stay? She knew the answer. Because he really felt nothing for her at all.

Sophie dreaded having to turn away and hesitated, prolonging the moment. The first forward step was the hardest but others somehow miraculously and automatically followed, widening the gap between them. It was agony not to indulge in one last look back at him. But she dared not. Drew was probably walking away already, too.

Thinking rationally, Sophie convinced herself she couldn't sacrifice her career for a dreamboat who had walked into her life and turned her heart upside down. If he had truly loved her, he would never have let her go. She had merely been a tropical romance.

Sophie walked outside into the warm sultry air, blindly following her fellow passengers. She stumbled up the steps into the aircraft, feeling abandoned and unloved, knowing she had been a fool and wondering how on earth she was supposed to get on with the rest of her life.

Chapter 9

Feeling drained after Drew's cold goodbye, Sophie sank into her seat on the plane. Woodenly, she realised she must dispel her infatuation. She was being sentimental, reading more into the brief relationship with Drew than actually existed.

She focused on the reasons pulling her back to Sydney. Her studies. Work. Her dream. If only to give her life meaning and purpose to move on from here.

The aircraft engines increased power and they taxied for take-off. She had fallen hopelessly in love with a man she must forget. She supposed a person could fall out of love again, that her strong feelings would fade. She forced her eyes closed, willing herself to forget, as if by doing so it would be that simple.

A lump constricted her throat and she quickly turned away to look out of the window as the jet pushed its way into the sky. The three hour flight proved far too much time to think. Upon arrival in Sydney, Sophie discovered her despondency unchanged by distance.

When they landed, it was raining and water trickled pathetically down the taxi windows as it drove to her flat. She placed a courtesy call to her mother to let her know she was back, then spent the following days moping. Her spirits sank and it was an effort to work on her thesis. Even the flat didn't feel like home any more. She was constantly engulfed with a grinding emptiness.

Every day when she checked the mail, she hoped the photographs would arrive but knew it was too soon. It was the sleepless nights Sophie hated the most. She prowled the tiny hallway in the dark and raided the refrigerator, all to no avail. Peace of mind still remained elusive. A blessed escape were the half days she waited tables in the café. The hours were filled with noise and people and time flew so fast she asked for extra shifts to cover her feelings of loss until she readjusted, but she would have given anything for the presence of just one other special person.

One morning at breakfast, Sophie finally took herself in hand and realised all this brooding was not doing her any good. Needing a change of scenery and craving the sea, she hit on a solution. The family beach house up at Pittwater north of the city.

She phoned a co-worker and arranged for her to take over her roster at the café for the rest of the week, then called her mother to inform her about her plans. The house was usually vacant, her parents too busy to use if often.

'When are you going up?' Sophie's mother sounded distracted as always, obviously preoccupied with her social and charity engagements.

'I'm leaving immediately.' Sophie's mind drifted to the luxurious family hideaway that she loved.

As she jammed her favourite casual clothes into a small bag, Sophie recalled all the childhood summers wandering along the beach, the restless waves that thundered in from the Pacific Ocean and the tang of salty air.

She headed off in her small second hand

car and edged her way through city traffic, driving north across Middle Harbour and along the Pittwater Road to the Barrenjoey Peninsula that separated the powerful ocean surf from a tranquil inlet and national park.

The house was on the beach side and, on arrival, Sophie drove down into the garage of a split-level dwelling nestled amid other exclusive homes in scenic bushland overlooking the South Pacific Ocean.

Upstairs, she dumped her bag on a comfortable chair in front of the unlit fireplace and made straight for the sliding doors on to the deck. As she opened them, she was confronted by an invigorating sea wind.

Within two days, Sophie realised coming to the beach house had made no difference and been yet another big mistake in her life. Her gloom returned and her concentration evaporated. This falling-out-of-love business was taking longer and proving harder than she thought.

As she walked along the beach later in her sneakers, kicking at a shell and jumping away from waves swirling up on to the sand, she remembered the warm, tropical waters lapping around her feet. Was it only a week ago? A stiff wind whipped the hair back from her face and she gazed reflectively out to sea. Each day since had been an endurance and seemed like an eternity. Time for her now stretched unbearably, with no purpose, ahead.

There were few other people about but, with an eerie premonition, Sophie stilled, sensing another closer presence. Turning, she narrowed her eyes and looked along the beach. She shook her head in disbelief and her mouth went dry. A soft, involuntary gasp escaped and she clutched her throat.

For a moment, she had been captured by a vision, an apparition. A sandy head of hair, a familiar agile walk. No. Impossible. She wanted the image so badly to be real, her mind was playing tricks. She tried to ignore the approaching figure but her eyes were drawn to him.

As the vision firmed, she gaped and her heart lurched when she recognised the man coming straight toward her with long, deliberate strides was Drew Mitchell! What was he doing here?

And how had he found her? Propelled by something stronger than logic, Sophie's feet began to move, carrying her closer to him. Her pace quickened until he was only metres away.

His face split into a long, lazy smile. 'You look surprised,' he drawled. 'Didn't you expect to see me again?

Trembling, Sophie stammered out, 'I...guess not.'

He slowly shook his head. 'Oh ye of little faith,' he chided, his voice deepening to irresistible. 'I'm hurt. Have you forgotten me already?'

Appalled at the thought, Sophie blurted out, 'Oh no, Drew, I could never forget you.'

As his smile broadened, Sophie realised she had been innocently trapped into the admission. They stood barely centimetres apart and she ached for his touch. His tender gaze never left her bewildered face as he handed her a large envelope.

'The photographs.' Distracted by his comment, Sophie accepted them, puzzled. 'I thought you were going to post them?'

'What gave you that idea?'

She frowned. 'At the airport, you said-'

'I said you would receive them in a week, remember?'

'Yes.' An excited thrill shot through her

body.

'I always planned to bring them down personally.'

'You did? Why?'

'Sophie, you silly goose. Do you really think I would have let you go?' He paused, adding softly, 'There's something very special between us, isn't there?'

His words were like a shower of warmth when the sun bursts from behind a cloud, and Sophie's heart sang. She nodded, looking down at her feet.

'You could at least have said something,' she berated him good-naturedly. 'Given me something to look forward to. How did you know I was up here?'

'I phoned your mother.'

'I'm surprised she told you. Brookfield's are notoriously private and wary of strangers.'

'I charmed her into telling me.'

'You do have that effect on women,' she confessed.

'Getting any work done?' he teased.

Sophie struggled to suppress a sheepish grin. 'No.'

A veil of hair fell across her face and Drew brushed it tenderly back over her shoulder. Sophie grew weak as he tilted her face upward and cupped her cheek in his palm.

'God, I've missed you so much, Sophie,' he murmured.

Hearing his words, Sophie grew weak and soppy, and would have gladly forgiven him anything, including making her miserable this past week. Their eyes absorbed each other in a smitten rapture that any person who had ever fallen in love would recognise.

'Sophie,' Drew said, 'my love for you is as deep as the ocean blue.'

Stunned by the revelation she had longed for, not to mention his romantically poetic turn of phrase, Sophie chuckled with delight. Drew's arms imprisoned her and she clung to him, nestled against his warmth and revelling in his security.

Eventually, he broke away and kissed her on the forehead then ran sensitive fingers over her face. When that was no longer enough for both of them and they could not bear the separation, their lips came together in a passionate kiss, infused with the depth of their love.

When they parted, Sophie felt as though

his kiss had brought her to life again and she had just recovered after a long illness.

'I have some incredible news,' Drew said, his dark eyes glowing. Intrigued, Sophie waited for elaboration but he merely said, 'Don't I get invited up to the house?'

Hand in hand, they scrambled back up the cliff path. Sophie made tea and they sat in padded cane chairs in the sitting room overlooking the ocean.

When Drew made no attempt to explain, she prompted, 'Don't keep me waiting any longer. What news?'

'All in good time,' he stalled her enthusiasm. 'First things first.'

'Such as?'

'Why I let you go and made you wait,' he said softly. 'I wanted to make certain you were really sure about your feelings. I thought time apart would give you a chance to consider them.'

Sophie dissolved beneath the liquid brown eyes but flashed him a murderous glare all the same, which he could never have misinterpreted as anything other than the fact that he was clearly in disgrace.

'You didn't come near me at the airport,' she accused.

'Darling.' He gently placed his hands on her shoulders. 'I didn't dare. If I'd touched you, I would never have let you go.' He glanced down at her pretended angry facade, hugged her tight and kissed her forehead. 'I ached for you. But I knew it would be selfish to pressure you. You had so much on your mind. But it wasn't until after your plane had taken off at Townsville that I realised I'd made the unforgivable mistake of never actually saying I loved you. I assumed you knew how I felt.'

'Well, I didn't.' Sophie pretended to be cross again.

He eyed her with genuine remorse. 'I never meant to hurt you.'

'Well, you did,' she gently chastised him. 'I've been desolate for a whole week. So, what are you going to do about it, Drew Mitchell?'

He traced the line of her mouth with his finger. 'Make amends.'

'Getting warm. How?'

'Apologise.'

She made him wait for a moment then wrinkled her nose. 'Oh, all right. Accepted. Then what?'

'Marry you, of course.' Sophie blushed

with delight. 'No man could do less. Besides,' he winked, 'Constance gave her blessing after our visit.' There was more than a hint of devilment in his voice.

'So that's why you took me there! You knew even then?' she ventured shyly and, with a sudden thought, added, 'What about your mother? I haven't met her yet.'

'She'll adore you.'

'So, since you have everything else organised, when are we getting married then?' she prompted, nestling closer, completely sure of him now.

'When you finish your thesis.'

Sophie groaned. 'It's still not finished.'

'Well, my news will give you motivation to finish and gain your qualification. For what I have in mind, you're going to need it.'

Sophie laughed. 'I don't believe you have any news at all. You're just teasing. Again.'

Drew's eyes twinkled with mischief. 'It's about our island.'

Our island. Sophie loved how that sounded. 'We don't have one yet,' she reminded him, excited that they could now work on their dream together.

'If it's all right with you, and I'm aware your share will be far greater than mine, I'd like to suggest we pool our resources.'

'Agreed.' She regarded Drew warily, intrigued as to where the conversation was leading. 'This is starting to sound awfully real. And not a little bit scary. Spill,' she urged impatiently.

Seeing he held her full attention, he began, 'Further north of Jewel Island is a smaller cay, never named and privately owned.'

Sophie's eyes immediately lit up with interest. 'Go on.'

'I'd heard of it but never went there until recently to check it out. It belonged to a man nicknamed Harry the Hobo who discouraged visitors. I'm not sure anyone ever knew his real identity or much about him. Apparently, he was a jaded professional and hated crowds. Fifty years ago, he dropped out of mainstream life, bought the island and basically became a beachcomber.'

'I can understand that,' Sophie said.

'He was also an extremely talented artist but unfortunately he died some months ago. His next of kin don't want the island so it's up for sale.'

Sophie's gaze widened. Drew reached for her hands and squeezed them tight. 'It's very small. Barely a blip on the reef but, honey, this is the opportunity of a lifetime. We have to try for it.'

She groaned. 'Do we have a chance? Some high roller might waltz in and snap it up.'

Drew shook his head. 'That's the best part. Everyone has equal standing. The island goes up for auction in two weeks and the advantage is it's too small to interest developers.'

The following fortnight dragged. For the first week, they stayed at the beach house together, Drew using the spare room, and cooking while Sophie worked madly on her thesis until her eyes bulged and her fingers ached from tapping on the laptop, to keep her mind occupied as much as to finish the project.

Drew proofread her manuscript and, with the benefit of his marine knowledge, suggested improvements and changes. Finally, it was done and Sophie delivered it to her professor at the university, anxious but relieved.

The second week, Drew returned to Queensland while Sophie headed back to Sydney, both of them making their own necessary final arrangements before the auction.

Eventually, the day of the auction arrived, conducted in a grand meeting room of the Stamford Plaza Hotel in Brisbane with stunning views over the city and the river, not that either Sophie or Drew was in any state of mind to enjoy their luxurious surroundings.

Surveying all the expensive suits and designer clothes around them, seated on plush chairs with thick dark carpet beneath their feet, Sophie cast a sceptical glance at Drew. They clasped each other's hands so tightly with tension, it hurt.

As the tedious minutes of the auction progressed, most other bidders lapsed and competition for the island dwindled to themselves and another single rival. When Sophie and Drew approached their budget limit, her hopes faded. Each second was agony but she gritted her teeth, determined to persist.

Drew nodded subtly to the auctioneer one last time. The room grew hushed, expectant.

'Going once.'

Sophie's heart pounded with excitement and she barely dared to breathe and wasn't game to glance over at their opposition.

'The bid is with the young couple over here, ladies and gentlemen.' The auctioneer pointed in their direction. He paused. 'Going twice.'

Sophie's stomach churned and Drew flashed her a stunning grin. She prayed all other bidding had ceased and she wouldn't see another subtle nod or raised hand.

'For the last time.'

The tension was unbearable. The auctioneer raised his hammer above the podium in front of the small select crowd and it descended with a thump.

'Sold!'

Ecstatic and knowing it was totally inappropriate in such an elegant setting, Sophie squealed and flung her arms around Drew's neck, then they sealed their success and future with a dynamic kiss.

That night over a celebratory dinner in the hotel restaurant, Drew asked, 'What did J.B. say when you told him of our plans to buy an island?'

Sophie recalled every single word of the strained telephone conversation. She was probably wrong but thought she perceived a hint of concession in her father's tone. An olive branch perhaps?

'He asked how on earth I expected to make a fortune chasing fish.' She laughed a little sadly and then sobered. 'I told him I'd be catching fish to eat, not to sell. I also told him I didn't need a fortune. Just a living.'

She sighed. 'I guess he didn't get where he is by being a saint. I think he has unwanted visions of his grandchildren running barefoot and naked along a beach.'

With enchanting magnetism, Drew threw back his head and laughed. 'They probably will, won't they?'

Three months later, Sophie Brookfield, heiress, and Drew Mitchell, charmer extraordinaire, barefoot and casual, were married on their own island beach. Witnessed and attended by a beaming Constance, a glowering J.B. Brookfield and his wife, Stephanie and their mother.

And to Sophie's ultimate joy, her nomadic brother, David, whom she had finally tracked down, returned briefly from the wilderness especially for the occasion.

***

The promised grandchildren soon arrived.

Two boys, Toby and Nick, and a girl, Lily. Who did, as toddlers, happily and innocently scamper about barefoot and naked, as predicted, shocking Sophie's parents but delighting Great Grandmother Constance who visited often, flown out from Cairns to Mitchell Cay by Drew in the helicopter.

Grandpa Brookfield kept his eye on the grandsons as potential Managing Directors but Sophie, knowing all of her children but especially her devilish water-baby sons only too well, just smiled secretly to herself and didn't like his chances.